PRETENSES

OTHER BOOKS BY KEITH LEE JOHNSON
Sugar & Spice
Fate's Redemption (Summer 2005)

PRETENSES

Keith Lee Johnson

A
SBI
PUBLICATION
A Strebor Books International LLC Publication
Distributed by Simon & Schuster, Inc.

Published by

Strebor Books International LLC
P.O. Box 1370
Bowie, MD 20718
http://www.streborbooks.com

ISBN 978-1-59309-018-0   ISBN 1-59309-018-8
LCCN 2003112280

This book is a work of fiction. Names, characters, places and incidents are products of the
author's imagination or are used fictitiously. Any resemblance to actual events or locales or
persons, living or dead, is entirely coincidental.

Distributed by Simon & Schuster, Inc.
1230 Avenue of the Americas
New York, NY 10020
1-800-223-2336

Cover art: © www.mariondesigns.com

First Printing June 2004
Manufactured and Printed in the United States

10 9 8 7 6 5 4 3 2 1

Praise for PRETENSES

"Keith Lee Johnson has worked his magic in this wonderfully written suspense thriller. *Pretenses* is packed with multi-layered suspenseful plots that will leave a reader thirsty for more. The name states it all as raw truths are revealed. Murder, deception, and betrayal—a must-read."

—Tee C Royal of RAWSISTAZ Book Club

"*Pretenses* is intriguing! I couldn't put it down. It moves quickly and had me guessing."

—Valorie M. Taylor, author of *Secrets of Gingerbread Men*

"Entertaining and suspenseful, Phoenix Perry is a heroine for the new millennium."

—Sibylla Nash, author of *Dream City*

"Keith Lee Johnson's novel, *Pretenses* is vivid, fast and thoughtfully paced, exciting, sobering. The action scenes and violence are especially brilliant. The whole work is written in a very lean prose while carrying some very important themes. There is a wealth of surprises and twists of plot to please the most demanding reader of this popular genre."

—James Cunningham, Dept. of English, University of Toledo

TO LILA THORNTON, WHO BELIEVED IN ME.
Your kind words of encouragement served as the rocket launcher
that ignited the flame and helped me write this book in 30 days.
Thanks for believing I could do it.

ACKNOWLEDGMENTS

To Him, who is able to do considerably more than I can ask or think; I give thanks.

To Kung Fu Master, Jeff Weasel of the Tiger's Den Martial Arts School, who taught me what little I know of the art, thank you.

To Leonard Kress, my fiction writing teacher at Owens Community College, your encouragement to write Life Choices way back in 1996 was very instrumental in launching my career. Thanks for telling me to finish that short story in your class. I'm often asked, "What made you start writing?" I have answered this question so many times that I've lost count. But I always tell the story about you and fellow professor, Shannon Smith, sitting in your cubicles, discussing that original short story that became a 579-page novel. I often wonder what would have happened if Shannon had not mentioned my short to you? Would I be an author today?

To Martina "Tee C" Royal of RAWSISTAZ Book Club, thanks for spreading the word and being a genuine source of encouragement.

To the dead (Bruce Lee, Malcolm X, Dr. Martin Luther King Jr.), your words and philosophies live on in me.

Special thanks to the Toledo Public Library for all its help researching this and other projects.

To fellow Toledoan Marcus Cordland, thanks for the use of your image. You helped bring Keyth to life.

To my editor, Sibylla Nash, author of *Dream City*, thanks for all the insight and a myriad of helpful questions on this and other projects. I'm looking forward to working with you again.

A very special thank you goes out to Police Officer Pamela Adrienne Wise-Wilson, who spread the word among her coworkers at 911 Emergency in Toledo, Ohio. You've been a huge help.

To Daryl Newsome, Dana Ingram, Bonnie Williams, Annie Toyer, Billie Kwiatkowski, Gail Washington, and my uncle Eddie Gray Hooker for purchasing Sugar & Spice and spreading the word.

To Roderick Vincent Allen, my best friend, and his father George Allen, who treated me like a son since I was fifteen years old, thanks for all the free barbeque from your restaurant in Toledo—Mister Big Stuff's Plantation Barbeque.

To Leonora Hunter, I appreciate all that you're doing in San Diego to help get my name out there in the wild, wild West.

To Trena Bell, founder of the Black Pearls Book Club in Dallas, Texas, thanks so much for picking me up at Love Field Airport and showing me a wonderful time while I was there in August 2003. I'm looking forward to meeting with you and all the pearls again.

A special thanks goes out to Professors Lorry Cology and Linda See, and all my teachers at Owens, for all of their encouragement.

Special, special thanks to Zane, Charmaine Parker, and Strebor Books International for diligently working behind the scenes on my behalf, making my dreams a tangible reality, for opening the door of opportunity, making all the BS I've been through with wannabes in the publishing arena (so-called agents, publishers [more than one] etcetera) WORTH IT ALL. I have struggled for seven years in relative obscurity, wanting to work with other black folk (not that I'm against working with whites) who had a vision of working together for once in our collective lives, and not be at one another's throats in the process. I fully understand that anything worth achieving will not be easy, but Zane, you, Charmaine, and Pamela Crockett have been a bright and burning light by which other African-American publishers can learn and model their own companies; putting such things as honesty first and actually paying your authors what's due them, and paying them on time without excuses, which indeed is truly the American way.

Special thanks to Camille and Romaine James, a set of identical African-American clairvoyant twins who predicted I would meet a woman (Zane) from the East and that that woman would help me become a big success. Well, Camille and Romaine, you young ladies predicted this nearly a year ago and half of your prediction has come to pass...How could I have forgotten to acknowledge you two sweet women? Please find it in your hearts to forgive me.

To Donna Garth, wife of one of my best friends, Fred, who took the time out of her busy schedule to read my mysteries, a genre she doesn't usually read. Thanks so much!

Thanks to Larry Whatley of the Urban Beat radio program in Toledo, Ohio. Thanks for the air time, my brother. We must do it again. I had so much fun. You let a brotha talk. And if you know me at all, I have to say what's on my mind. Thanks!

PROLOGUE
CHAPTER 1

9400 Mount Vernon Circle
Alexandria, Virginia
June 2001

A FIGURE, dressed in a black uniform, nested in a tree across the street from the house, waiting for Supreme Court nominee Jennifer Taylor to arrive. It was all so perfect. No one would be able to figure out the real reason Jennifer and Webster Taylor had been murdered. Influenced by the media hype, people might assume that they were murdered because of their opposition to abortion, which had nothing to do with it. Something far more shocking was going on. The Taylors would be the first of a long list of people to be killed. But none of that mattered now. The loving couple would be dead in a few minutes.

If necessary, the figure would have stayed in the tree until dawn, remaining perfectly still, hidden by the foliage. From the comfortable perch, the figure was able to scrutinize every car that entered the cul-de-sac.

At 11:00, Judge Taylor's black Mercedes-Benz cruised quietly up the street and turned into the driveway. Immediately, the figure jumped from the tree when the automatic garage door began to open and ran across the street. Judge Taylor hit the door button and entered the house without waiting for the automatic door to close completely. The figure walked into the garage, breaking the motion detector beam. The garage door stopped descending and automatically reversed.

Webster Taylor sat in front of the television set in the living room cheering on the Los Angeles Lakers.

"Who's winning, Web?" the figure heard the Supreme Court nominee ask her husband.

The figure could see the long-legged, fifty-five-year-old beauty who had no idea the figure was stealthily creeping toward her. The carpeted hallway absorbed the sound of footsteps as the figure tiptoed further and further. A few more steps and the figure would be within reach of the controversial judge.

"My Lakers! Kobe Bryant is having a field day. How'd the meeting go?"

"Terrible. We can talk about it after the game."

The figure entered the living room, kicked Judge Taylor in the back of her knee with a powerful thrust kick, and then grabbed a hunk of her thick hair and jerked sharply to the right, snapping her neck like a twig. Jennifer Taylor grunted a little just before taking her last breath.

Hearing the sound, Webster turned around to see what had happened to his wife. He saw a figure dressed in black holding a semiautomatic with a silencer attached to the muzzle. "Oh, no," he said with resignation, just before a single bullet pierced his forehead. The Assassin picked up the expelled shell casing, walked swiftly back down the hallway and out through the garage, and disappeared into the night.

CHAPTER 2

THE RAPIST began his career following an incident on the Beltway. Apparently, he wasn't driving fast enough for the rude couple in the Lexus behind him. The man kept flashing his bright lights and blowing the horn. After the Rapist switched lanes to allow them to pass, the woman pressed her middle finger against the passenger side window as they sped by him.

The Rapist was so enraged that he followed them to the John F. Kennedy Concert Hall on F Street. The Royal Philharmonic Orchestra was performing. He asked the box office clerk what time the concert would be over and then returned to his car to wait. As the hours passed, his anger smoldered, growing more intense with each passing second. When the performance ended, people came out of the hall by the hundreds. The Rapist spotted the rude couple getting into their Lexus and followed them again. He was planning to teach them a lesson they would never forget.

The couple stopped at Marcel's restaurant on Pennsylvania Avenue, about a half-mile away from the Kennedy Center, for French cuisine. Marcel's normally closed at eleven, but all the restaurants were staying open late because of the concert. The Rapist was lucky enough to get a table next to the rude couple, which was only a few feet from the baby grand piano near the bar.

The Rapist sipped his coffee and pretended to read a copy of *The Washington Post*. He listened to the couple as they went on and on about the concert and how great the conductor was. He assumed they were married, judging by the wedding rings they wore. When they finished their meal, they talked quietly about going home to make love.

The Rapist followed them to their home in Alexandria, pulling into their driveway right behind them—flashing his bright lights into their eyes. Walking up to the driver's side window, he brandished a gun. The fear in their eyes exhilarated him when he realized they had completely forgotten the incident on the Beltway and had no idea who he was.

"I've got $300 in my billfold. Take it. It's yours," the man offered. "Take your ring off, honey. It's insured."

"I'm not a thief," the Rapist said. "Now get outta the fuckin' car."

At gunpoint, he forced the couple into the house and into the bedroom. He forced the wife to tape her husband's hands and feet with duct tape that he had brought with him. Feeling in complete control, the Rapist reminded them of the Beltway incident. The shock on their faces gave him a potent erection. He began to throb.

"This is gonna be a night to remember. I guarantee you that," the Rapist said gleefully. He looked at the woman, who was so terrified that she seemed to be frozen solid. "You two need a lesson in highway etiquette," he told them. "Strip, you high-class bitch."

She apologized profusely. "I'm sorry. Please…don't."

"Too late, sweetheart," the Rapist bluffed. He just wanted to scare them—push the situation to the limit, and leave them humiliated.

But the husband, believing that his wife was about to be raped, yelled, "I'll fucking kill you if you touch her!"

The Rapist laughed as the husband continued screaming, "You son-of-a-bitch! Touch her, and I'll hunt you down if it takes the rest of my life!"

When the wife was completely nude, the Rapist taped her limbs to the bedposts. He pulled out a switchblade and cut the tape away from the husband's hands and feet. Then he closed the knife and put it into his pocket. He tossed the gun to the other side of the room. "Okay, tough guy. Fucking kill me."

The husband, an upper-class professional who had gone to elite schools all of his life, was no match for the Rapist. After giving him a fierce pummeling, the Rapist tossed the husband on the bed and stripped his pants off.

"Oh, no! No! No! Please! Don't!" the husband whimpered, but it did no good. "Aaaaah!"

Moments later, the bed springs howled as the violation escalated to a feverish pace. The wife turned her eyes away, but she couldn't shut out the sound of her husband's screams.

After the Rapist had finished with the husband, he cut the tape away from the wife's hands and feet. "I was only gonna scare you, you rude motherfucker. But you had to be tough. You brought this shit on yourself. You fuckin' hear me! This was your fault. Not mine."

Then he watched the wife console her whimpering husband. Tears also ran down her cheeks. Standing over the weeping couple, the Rapist felt a sense of power that he had never felt before—it pleased him.

He left the couple to lick their wounds in their mutual humility. Later, when he thought about it, he realized that a strange thing had happened to him. The fight with the husband had been an aphrodisiac. Raping the husband had been the most fulfilling sex he had ever had.

★★★

During the next two years, the Rapist sexually assaulted sixty-seven men, none of whom ever reported the assaults to the police. They had no idea that a vicious rapist was at large until Father Merle Reynolds—his latest victim—told his story.

The traumatized priest was taken to the hospital where he told two detectives about the violent assault. The Rapist had come to St. Mary's Cathedral under the pretense of seeking absolution.

Before violating the priest, the Rapist, in vivid detail, had confessed all of his crimes, describing each victim by name and occupation. The priest, however, refused to divulge the names of the victims, citing the sanctity of the confessional, but told the detectives that the Rapist had given him permission to inform them of his existence and warn them that he intended to continue ravaging men at every opportunity.

PART 1
COCO NIMBURU

CHAPTER 3

I FELT THE presence of the two FBI agents who had just entered my dojo. I recognized the cologne of agent Patrick Flynn. That meant that the other presence I felt was that of his partner, Dick Ford. Something terrible must have happened for them to contact me when I was off duty.

I was going to have to return to my day job as FBI Special Agent in Charge Phoenix Perry. But first, I had something far more important to think about—my mind and body in perfect harmony. I was making a videotape of my training session with four of my best student-teachers. We were sparring at full speed, and each student-teacher was armed with a lethal weapon.

As a Grandmaster of Shaolin Kung Fu, I knew I had to take it easy on them, but not too easy. They had all earned the rank of black sash, but if I didn't use at least fifty percent of my chi, they wouldn't push themselves to master the art. For safety purposes, I had told them that once they were knocked down or were off the mat, they were considered knocked out and could no longer participate.

Armed with two knives, Earl Johns, the most aggressive of the four, lunged forward. I spun toward him faster than he could bat an eye. His knife just missed me, and I back-fisted him in the forehead. As he fell, I could feel a fighting stick coming at the back of my head, and I ducked out of the way.

The three remaining student-teachers were in front of me now. I advanced toward Valerie Ryan, who had a chain. Sensing when she would swing, I angled in to the left and hit her with a palm strike to the sternum just as she started her swinging motion. She flew backward about five feet with the chain still in her hand. Had I hit her anywhere above the shoulders, she would have been seriously injured.

Greg Fisher swung a staff at my ankles. He had the best technique, but he wasn't the best fighter. I jumped just high enough for the staff to pass under my feet. Then dropping to one knee, I spun around and swept both of Greg's legs out from under him. He fell hard onto the mat, and his staff flew up in the air. I caught it and spun it like a majorette twirling a baton.

Only Karen Monroe, who was close to mastering the art, remained. I initiated the joust by feinting at her feet. She came forward, rapidly swinging a pair of fighting sticks. We attacked back and forth without success for either of us. Then I waited for her to come forward again. When she did, I hit her wrist with Greg's staff, knocking one stick out of her hand. I could tell from her eyes that she was wondering, with her level of training, how such a simple move could have worked.

Seeing another opening, I knocked the other stick out of her hand, partly to show her it wasn't luck, but mainly to satisfy my own vanity. Having disarmed her, I tossed the staff away and advanced, throwing a series of quick strikes and kicks. My attack was fast but nowhere near as fast as it could have been. The idea was to lull the opponent into a rhythm and then break that rhythm by striking at full speed. I closed the distance between us. Then, without thought, I stepped in and delivered a powerful palm strike to Karen's chest, which sent her sailing across the room.

The match was over almost as quickly as it had begun. In less than two minutes and with minimal effort, I had dispensed with four armed Kung Fu artists. The student-teachers and I bowed to one another.

"What are the pillars of our philosophy?" I asked them.

In unison they said, "Emptiness, awareness, fluidity, totality, simplicity."

"Where do these lead us?"

"To freedom."

"Where does freedom lead us?"

"To no technique and to all technique."

I turned to Karen Monroe. "You were thinking about the simplicity of the move I executed in disarming you of the first stick when you lost the second, weren't you?"

Her head dropped. "Yes."

"What should you have done?" I asked, giving her a chance to learn from the mistake.

"I should have trusted my feelings. Somehow I knew what you were going to do. And when you did it, I was surprised at how simple it was."

"Good. You are not far from true freedom."

Addressing all the student-teachers, I said, "How many of you felt the presence of the two FBI agents behind me?"

Startled, they looked over my shoulders and saw the two men dressed in dark suits and ties. Then they looked at each other, wondering if anyone knew other than me.

"When true freedom has been attained, you will know without knowing." I let what I had just taught them sink in for a moment or two before I dismissed my students. "Okay, I'll see you all next week."

I faced Flynn and Ford and asked, "What's happened?"

CHAPTER 4

THE FBI had already taken over the investigation at the Taylor house, which enraged the local police. As far as they were concerned, FBI agents were always infringing on their territory, throwing their weight around, and taking all the credit for the success of an investigation. By the time I arrived, there was a mob scene in front of the house. Squad cars were everywhere. Flashing red and blue lights bounced off every vehicle and house in the vicinity. Satellites had been set up—reporters circled like vultures.

It was an unseasonably chilly Thursday night in June, so I grabbed my black FBI windbreaker and put it on as I was still wearing my Kung Fu uniform, and I wanted to look the part of a bona fide FBI agent. I got out of my metallic-green Ford Mustang Cobra and walked up the driveway.

I spotted Assistant Director Lawrence Michelson—a former boyfriend ten years removed—talking to the police. Michelson was a handsome black man, six feet tall, and extremely well-groomed. As a twenty-six-year-old agent, I had fallen under his spell. He was still obsessed with me, probably because I had married Keyth Perry, a former agent he didn't like.

I had broken it off with Lawrence when I learned that he was telling agents in the Washington office that he was going to be my first lover. Lawrence Michelson and I were never intimate, but most of the male agents believed the rumors. I remained a virgin until the night of my honeymoon.

When a female agent's reputation has been compromised, the word spreads like wildfire through the bureau. By breaking up with Lawrence as soon as I heard the rumors, I could at least retain some dignity while I did the job I enjoyed so much. Nevertheless, the rumors persisted, and Keyth, who had by then become my boyfriend, had to endure undeserved ridicule. All the tension eventually led to a fistfight with Lawrence, ending Keyth's career with the bureau.

Lawrence spotted me and came down the driveway.

"Perry," he called. He always addressed me by my last name in public. He was so good at pretenses. All the agents noticed that he gave me a hard time, and they knew why. Lawrence seemed to forget that trained agents accustomed to watching people noticed the subtlest hint of impropriety. "Why didn't you change before you came here?"

"Flynn and Ford said you wanted me here immediately."

"Flynn and Ford," he repeated, shaking his head. "Two numskulls who shouldn't even be agents. I didn't tell them you couldn't take time to change. They knew the fucking media was here."

"Maybe they were concerned with solving the crime, sir."

"Don't get flippant with me, Perry," he growled. "This is a career-making case, if you're up for the challenge."

"I'd rather catch the bad guys, Lawrence." He hated it when I called him that in public, but no one was around to hear it. I loved pushing his buttons. "Besides, I thought catching the Rapist was the high-priority case, Lawrence."

"Agent Perry, you will address me as Assistant Director Michelson. You got that? And you'll work whatever case I assign you to."

"Yes, sir!" I smiled and saluted. "Just a friendly reminder, Assistant Director Michelson. He isn't raping women. He's raping men. It's your ass on the line, not mine. No pun intended. But whatever you say, sir. What do we know so far?"

"Not much. We know they were killed sometime Wednesday night." He frowned. "The bodies were found by a neighbor who came by when she noticed the garage door had been open all day. Apparently, they never leave their garage door open."

"I'm gonna need to talk to her," I said.

"Perry, solving this case quickly is important to the president, which means it's important to the bureau. Director St. Clair said that President Davidson was furious when he found out about Taylor's murder. Her seat on the bench was very important to him, and apparently, he and Justice Patterson had carefully orchestrated her appointment."

"Her nomination was important to all of us. It's not like a black woman gets a presidential appointment to the Supreme Court every election."

"The Rapist case is on the back burner for now," Michelson said. "Find this bastard, Perry. The sooner the better."

CHAPTER 5

KELLY MCPHERSON'S shiny black Stingray was coming down the street—its hot-rod engine growling softly. Even with the windows up, I could hear Tupac Shakur's "Heartz of Men" playing loudly. Kelly had recruited me from Howard University, where I had earned my master's degree in criminology. After I graduated from the FBI academy in Quantico, Kelly trained me in the field. As a personal favor, I trained her in the martial arts. After five years of hard work, she was awarded a black sash in Kung Fu. I was proud to present it to her.

Kelly McPherson was tall, blonde, and very good-looking. She often downplayed her looks because men were constantly making unwanted advances. She wore loose-fitting clothing and no makeup, yet men still made attempts. In addition, there were those who thought that since she was so good-looking, she was getting by on her looks and couldn't be depended on in a fire fight, which wasn't true. Over time, Kelly had proven herself an excellent FBI agent.

She had earned the respect of her peers by backing them in fistfights and shoot-outs, and eventually she was promoted to Special Agent in Charge. Kelly helped pave the way for women like me to join the bureau. When Kelly first became an FBI agent, the bureau hierarchy introduced her as "one of our female agents." In response, she would frown and look down at her breasts. Kelly loved being an FBI agent, but she had seen too many good agents disciplined or fired for what she thought were minor infractions. When a liaison position with D.C. Metro was offered to her, she seized it. I hated to see her go, but when she took that position, Director St. Clair offered me the position she had vacated.

"It's about time you showed up," I said.

"Oh, hush. You probably just got here yourself." She laughed and jogged up the driveway. "Must be some real big ass to kiss on this case, huh, Michelson?"

Michelson frowned and then barked, "We don't have time for your bullshit, McPherson! Yours either, Perry. I want this solved and solved quickly."

"Assistant Director Michelson," I said, trying to bring some levity to the situation, "you will address me as Special Agent in Charge Perry."

Michelson stared at me for a few moments, trying not to laugh. Kelly said, "Somebody's in need of a serious blowjob."

Michelson laughed at Kelly's glib retort. Even though she occasionally got under his skin, he often welcomed her comic relief. "Okay, playtime is over. Get to work and make us all look good. Or somebody's head is coming off at the shoulders."

CHAPTER 6

THE BODIES were still being photographed when I entered the Taylor house. Flynn and Ford had already briefed me on the crime scene, so I knew that powerful hands had broken Judge Taylor's neck, which meant the assailant was probably a man. What bothered me was that Webster Taylor was shot in the forehead. As I looked down at Webster, I wondered why the killer hadn't shot them both.

Was Webster's murder personal? Was that why he was shot in the head? Or was Judge Taylor's death personal? This is strange. Did the killer or killers take some pleasure in killing Judge Taylor? If so, maybe we should start by looking into some of her cases. Find out who might hold a grudge.

I had spoken with the neighbor who had found them. According to her, she had seen Webster watching an NBA playoff game around 9:30 the previous evening through the Taylors' large picture window. She went on to tell me that the Taylors were perfectly suited for each other, sharing a love of books, theater, art, romantic movies, the symphony, and the law. The couple had celebrated their silver anniversary recently, and they were still very much in love. Judge Taylor had told her that she and her husband had planned to make some popcorn and watch the basketball game that evening. Later, they planned to get into the Jacuzzi, which overlooked Dogue Creek, and watch the stars.

They had so much to look forward to, I thought. In just four days, Jennifer Taylor's confirmation hearing would have begun. If confirmed, she would have been only the third woman to sit on the Supreme Court. According to Michelson, retiring Justice Patterson had handpicked her as his replacement. President Harrison Palmer Davidson, Patterson's college roommate and best friend, was a year-and-a-half shy of finishing his second term and wanted to appoint one more justice to the bench before he left office.

A media firestorm ensued the day President Davidson made Patterson's replacement known. Judge Taylor was a very vocal conservative who didn't support abortion on demand. The court was currently split on the abortion issue, with Justice Street, a moderate who often voted conservatively, carrying the deciding vote. Women's rights organizations were furious. Angry women picketed in front of the White House daily, carrying signs that read, "Abort Taylor!"

The most demonstrative group was led by a militant feminist named Patricia English. Patricia had remained silent about Taylor's stance on abortion, but when President Davidson nominated Taylor to replace Justice Patterson, Patricia organized an all-out attack on her qualifications.

"Anyone ever tell you, you look just like Jada Pinkett?" a Secret Service agent asked me.

"Tell me, what do you think of all of this?" I asked him, avoiding the question I'd heard much too often. It really annoyed me to be asked that question constantly.

"I think I'd like to ask you out on a date," he replied, trying to charm me.

I looked at him. He was a tall black man, with a thick, neatly trimmed mustache. He smiled. I could tell he was too impressed with himself and probably used his Secret Service credentials to get dates. "You ever work a murder scene before?"

He shook his head.

"Then what the hell are you doing here?" I snarled.

"The president wanted one of our guys here. I'm Agent Andrew Jordan. My friends call me A.J."

"Agent Jordan, if you don't know what's going on, get the hell outta the way. This is a crime scene, not a pickup bar."

He looked around to see who might have heard my rancorous comment, then rolled his eyes, said something into the microphone tucked into his right sleeve, and left the area.

Kelly was examining Judge Taylor's body. "You getting any vibes, Kelly?" I called out.

"Yeah, I'm thinking this is strange, Phoenix," she called back. "Come and look at this."

I went over to Judge Taylor's body to see what she was talking about. By the time I got there, everyone had come over to see. Kelly lifted the judge's right leg. There was a huge bruise in the back of her knee.

"What do you think, Phoenix?" Kelly asked.

"She was hit pretty damn hard. I wonder if that's the only bruise on her body. I wonder if the husband also has bruises. They could have been tortured for information. Only way to find out is to treat this like either one of them could have been the target."

"I agree," Kelly said.

I checked the caller ID, which showed 112 calls. The calls went back as far as December. Using her cell, Kelly called the bureau to get one of the techs to pull up the Taylors' home and office telephone records.

"Kelly, we better check their cell phone logs, too," I said.

CHAPTER 7

I MADE IT HOME just in time to walk Savannah, my six-year-old daughter, to Matthew Henson Academy. The school was the main reason we had moved into the Arlington area. Henson was one of a few private schools that required students not only to attend year-round but to commit to being there on Saturdays also. Consequently, most of the students were two or three grades above the norm. Savannah never missed a day of school.

I was supposed to meet Director St. Clair at the White House by eleven o'clock. Director St. Clair had wanted me to be there when he briefed President Davidson at his regular 8:00 meeting, but I insisted on coming home first. There wasn't anything significant to report on the Taylor homicides yet. On a case like this, there was no telling how many hours I would have to work. I was already spending a lot of hours on the Rapist case. While it was an honor to meet with the President under any circumstances, I wanted to walk my daughter to school as often as possible.

Savannah leaped into my arms the moment I opened the door.

"Hi, Mommy!"

"Hi, precious." I kissed her on the cheek.

"Look, Mommy. See how Daddy dressed me?" She was wearing one of three uniforms that the Matthew Henson Academy required. The school's colors were green and gold. Savannah looked so adorable in her uniform. Keyth had even put a green-and-gold ribbon in her hair.

"Did you eat breakfast, honey?"

"Yeah." She smiled. "Me and Daddy made it together."

"Did you eat it all?"

"Uh-huh."

"Okay, honey. I need to talk to your daddy for a second. Then I'll walk you to school, okay?"

Keyth, who looked like Midwest model Marcus Cordland, had just gotten out of the shower when I walked into the bedroom. He was drying himself off, unaware that I was staring lustfully at his muscular back. My eyes dropped to his delicious ass. It was the shape of a round doughnut. I wanted to take a bite. Even after eight years of marriage, he still turned me on.

"You in a hurry to get to the office?" I asked him.

He turned around, and I got a full frontal view of his sculptured physique.

"How long have you been here?" he asked.

"Long enough to know I need taking care of before you go to work."

He smiled. I kissed him, grabbing as much of his ass as I could get into my small hands. At 6 feet 3 inches, Keyth was seven inches taller than me. We started kissing, and his lips tasted good. I could smell fresh cinnamon on his breath.

He pulled away. "You better get on outta here and take Savannah to school, girl."

"Okay. Kiss me again before I go."

"Mommy, come on," Savannah called out from the hallway. "You gon' make me late for school."

CHAPTER 8

I PRACTICALLY DRAGGED Savannah to school and hurried home. There was a river between my legs. Keyth pulled me in and closed the door. First he pulled off my uniform jacket, then the tee shirt I wore underneath. He flicked his tongue over my nipples and I lost control. I took him, right there, on the floor, in the foyer. Then we climbed in the shower and he washed my back.

Totally relaxed, I found myself thinking about the case, still wondering who the intended victim was. Keyth was talking to me, but I had no idea what he was saying. I didn't mean to ignore him, but I couldn't shake the thought of that mark on Judge Taylor's leg. Somehow, I knew it was the key to understanding what had really happened that night. But what kind of weapon had been used and why?

"Are you listening to me?" Keyth asked.

"I'm sorry, baby. No. I was thinking about the Taylor case."

"That's what I was asking you about. What do you think happened?"

"Deep down?"

"Yeah. Deep down."

"For some reason, I think the killer wanted or needed to kill Judge Taylor with his bare hands. What I can't figure out is who wanted her dead. Was it someone from one of the radical feminist groups angry over the abortion issue? Or was it someone who had appeared before her?"

"Have you given much consideration to the husband being the target?"

"Yes, but the man was a lawyer. Who would have wanted him dead?"

"Probably a lot of people." Keyth laughed.

"Guess what?" I asked.

"What?"

"I'm going to meet the President."

CHAPTER 9

WHITE HOUSE Chief of Staff Armando Glover asked me if I was ready to meet the President of the United States. We were standing outside the Commander in Chief's office. It was an awesome question. How many Americans actually meet the President in the Oval Office?

I was wearing an olive suit, a white blouse, and olive shoes. I looked myself over in the small makeup mirror I carried in my purse.

"You look like a million bucks," Chief Glover told me.

I didn't feel like a million bucks, but the compliment felt good. I took a deep breath and nodded to the Chief of Staff. He opened the door for me, and I stepped onto the thick navy blue carpet. Suddenly, I was nervous. The president was talking to Director St. Clair.

"Special Agent Perry, the President of the United States," Chief Glover said.

The president shook my hand firmly and led me to a chair in front of his desk.

"No need to be nervous, Agent Perry." He smiled. "Director St. Clair tells me that Sydney Drew is your father."

Presidents always have their researchers find out small, almost insignificant details about the people meeting them for the first time. It makes the visitor feel important.

"Yes."

"They tell me he used to work for the National Security Agency," the President went on. "So what's he doing now?"

"He runs the Drew Perry Investigative Firm with my husband, Keyth, sir."

"Nothing wrong with putting the training we gave him to good use." He chuckled. "Tell me, what do you think about this case?"

"Well, sir, we don't have much to go on, but I'm sure Director St. Clair told you that this morning."

"He did. But what I'm interested in now is what you've extrapolated from the crime scene. What's your best guess, Phoenix?"

"I think the judge was the target. I haven't gotten any results from the crime lab yet, but Webster Taylor doesn't have any bruises on him. And since he doesn't, then he was probably killed just because he was there."

President Davidson folded his arms and leaned against his desk. "Do you think any hate groups are involved?"

"Unlikely, sir."

"Why not?" He seemed disappointed.

"Hate groups want you to know they did it and why. And none of them are taking credit for the murders—not yet anyway. But I'll check them out anyway, sir."

He looked at his watch. "In about five minutes I'm going to have a press conference on the White House lawn. I'm going to introduce you as the person running the show. The press is going to have many questions, and there will be lots of pressure on you, Phoenix. Can you handle it?"

"Certainly, sir, but it's always been the bureau's policy to let someone from the public relations office handle the press."

"I know, but today is going to be different," he said with determination. "A lot of people didn't want Taylor on the court because she was black. Did you know that, Phoenix?"

"No, sir, I didn't. But I'm not surprised." I hadn't meant to say that last part, but it had found its way out of my mouth.

"That's another reason I requested you to work this case. I want the killer to know that I will not be thwarted."

Oh, great. Now I'm going to be put on parade for the cause.

"I want a black woman right up there with me. I want them to see that this administration is going to find and promote well-qualified minorities and put them in positions where their strengths and talents can do the most good for this nation."

CHAPTER 10

COCO NIMBURU of the notorious Nimburu clan had been conditioned and trained in the ninja fighting arts since she was five years old. The Nimburu clan had existed for five-hundred years. They were only one of a few sects that survived the 1581 ninja slaughter in feudal Japan. In those days, the Nimburus were so vicious that when it was known that a Nimburu was assigned to kill a particular person, the victim often killed himself to avoid the savage death that awaited him.

Coco was a master of disguise and could speak many languages and dialects, including French, Russian, German, Vietnamese, Arabic, English, Mandarin, Cantonese, and Japanese. Her unique talent with languages enabled her to travel the world, carrying out assassinations for whomever could afford to pay the hefty sum her special skills commanded. On this assignment, she had booked two rooms on different floors at the Capitol Hill Hyatt Regency.

She finished practicing her deadly art and her stretching routine, showered, and turned on the television. She watched the FOX News channel to find out what the police were saying about the Taylor murders. Law enforcement officials could always be counted on to tip their hands about an investigation.

President Davidson was shown standing behind a lectern that had the presidential seal on it. A barrage of lights flashed as he spoke. Coco turned up the sound to hear what he was saying. Davidson did not attempt to appear presidential. His anger gushed forth when he opened his mouth.

"No assassination, no intimidation, and no organization of any kind will discourage this White House from naming a nominee of my choosing to a seat on the Supreme Court!" Davidson said abruptly. "We are determined, I say we are determined, to apprehend everybody involved in the murder of Jennifer and Webster Taylor! There is no place you can run, no place you can hide. We will find you, whoever you are, and bring you to justice!" He paused and glanced at the press. "Your questions will be answered by one of the FBI's best and brightest, Special Agent Phoenix Perry."

The name triggered something in Coco's memory. Grabbing her laptop, she pulled up the hit-list file and scanned it for the name she had just heard. There it was. Sydney Drew of Drew Perry Investigative Firm. Coco wondered if it could be a coincidence. If it wasn't, she might have to kill an FBI agent. In her line of work, innocent people were often killed for being in the wrong place at the wrong time. The last thing she wanted was to murder an FBI agent, but if it was necessary, so be it. She pointed the remote control at the television and pushed the power button.

Coco decided to get into her disguise. She would be meeting NSA Director Clayton Pockets downstairs in the lounge in about an hour. He had a thing for blondes, so she would become one for him. Seduction was always a good weapon when used by a skilled practitioner. Coco had used her charms on men and women alike; both were extremely susceptible if the seduction was alluring enough, and Coco Nimburu was.

Dressed in her disguise, she entered the lounge. The dim lighting would hide what she looked like when the FBI asked for a description, and Coco didn't want that. She wanted to be seen. Clayton Pockets smelled her intoxicating perfume before he actually saw her. She reminded him of the character that Drea De Matteo had brought to life on HBO's *The Sopranos*. Wearing a skintight white tennis outfit, sneakers, hoop earrings, and a bright smile, she said loudly with a New York accent, "You must be Director Pockets. Here," she handed him the blackmail money he was owed, "this is for you." She cracked the gum she was chewing a few times before turning to walk away.

"Hey, what's the rush?" Pockets asked. "Can't you stay for a drink?"

As she turned back, Coco noticed that everyone was staring at her, which was exactly what she wanted. That way they could tell the FBI what she looked like.

"I've got a better idea. How 'bout we take that briefcase and get outta here. I know a great spot for a little fun about fifteen minutes from here, in Alexandria."

"Great!" He smiled broadly. "Just let me tell the office I'm taking the rest of the afternoon off."

"I'll wait for you in the parking lot," Coco said and left.

A couple of minutes later, Clayton Pockets came into the parking lot, carrying the briefcase Coco had given him. She was sitting on a black, yellow-trimmed ninja motorcycle. She wasn't wearing a helmet. He walked over to her and said, "So what's your name, sweet thing?"

"My name?" she repeated, and cracked her gum a few times. "My name is Coco, and I know how to make a man have repeated orgasms without losing his erection."

Intrigued, Pockets asked, "How?"

"Ever try acupuncture?" She smiled, then remained silent to allow the suggestion to flood his mind. She kick-started the bike and revved the engine a few times. "Try to keep up with me. If you get lost, it's your loss." Then she peeled off. The smell of rubber burning filled Pockets' nose. He ran to his car and pursued her.

CHAPTER 11

POLICE HEADQUARTERS was always busy. Today wasn't any different. There was no end to crime in the nation's capital. Many of the poorer neighborhoods were littered with drugs and, consequently, violence. It was dog-eat-dog not far from where the President slept. The moment I walked in, prisoners began their ritualistic catcalls. I had grown tired of the constant offers of sex from incarcerated men. Most of them were quite bold, too. On one occasion, a prisoner exposed himself so I could see what he had to offer.

"Hey, baby," one of the shabbier ones said to me. "You look just like Jada Pinkett. You think you can handle this?" I ignored him and kept walking. Then he yelled out, "Ah, come on, girl! Don't be like that. All I want is a taste. You can have it right back. I promise." He laughed uproariously.

I walked into Kelly's office with a frown on my face. She was sitting at her desk, looking at the Taylors' telephone records. I opened her portable refrigerator and took out a big, juicy-looking peach.

"You're welcome," Kelly said.

"Don't mind if I do." I laughed.

"Saw the press conference this afternoon. The President has all kinds of confidence, doesn't he?

"Yeah, but it's misplaced."

"You thinkin' what I'm thinkin'?"

"Yeah. What if it was a pro?"

"Exactly. And if it was, he's gone." Kelly shook her head. "And the President is on the television sellin' wolf tickets. Writing checks your ass may end up cashing."

"I know. Ain't life grand?"

"It sure is. Look, this is what I got. While you were at home getting your swerve on with Keyth, I was doing some real police work." She flashed a smile. "It turns out that four of the calls came from the Four Seasons Hotel the day she was murdered."

"Yeah?" I said, looking at the circled numbers on the print-out.

"Judge Taylor's cell phone records show that she called the hotel. I think we oughta get over there. With any luck, whoever called the judge may still be checked in."

"Let's go." Once the trail was cold, we would never catch the killer.

"But first the D.C. police want you to do them a small favor, Phoenix."

"Yeah, anything for the boys in blue."

"They brought a bad-ass wife beater in here earlier." Kelly opened a drawer and pulled out several photos. I cringed when I saw his handiwork. "He's not your typical coward either. The son-of-a-bitch beat the shit outta five officers. It took two tasers to take him down and ten patrolmen to bring him in."

"PCP?"

Kelly shook her head. "Just one bad hombre."

"Where is he?"

"In Interview One."

"Let's go."

I walked into the interview room totally focused yet with my mind clear, relaxed, and completely in tune with the danger in the room. Emotions like anger shut down a martial artist's senses, and we become vulnerable.

The prisoner looked at me and smiled just a little. Both of his hands were cuffed to the table. He had a bald head, jailhouse tattoos on his arms, and a body he had no doubt built at Lorton Prison.

"Gentlemen, I need to speak with you in the hall," Kelly said. "Special Agent Perry will stay with the prisoner."

"Uncuff him," I said calmly.

"Are you sure?" one of the officers said, playing along.

"Yeah," I said, tossing my peach in the air and catching it. "He seems calm now. You won't bite, will you?"

"Naw." He laughed. "I won't bite."

The officers left quietly, but I knew they practically ran to the observation room next door where a crowd of officers had gathered when they learned that I was in the building. They wanted to beat the crap out of him themselves, but if it ever leaked out, which these things were prone to do, the media would have a field day. But I'm a woman, and I only weigh 125 pounds. What was he going to say? A woman kicked my ass? Even if he wanted to, his pride wouldn't let him.

The prisoner was quietly looking back and forth from the unlocked door to me, calculating his chances of escape. I kept tossing my peach in the air and catching it. After a couple of minutes, he said, "So...what, you FBI, or somethin'?"

"Uh-huh," I muttered, watching his every move.

"So when they comin' back?"

"About twenty minutes or so, I'd say."

"So...you got a gun or somethin'?"

"Nope."

"If they gon' be gone for twenty minutes, what's tuh stop me from walkin' the fuck outta here?"

"Just little ol' me." I smiled.

"What? With no gun? You crazy." He laughed. "Did they tell you I sent five of D.C.'s finest to Washington Memorial this mornin', tryin' tuh mess wit' me?"

"Yeah, they told me."

"And you still came in here, huh?" He frowned. "You must be one bad bitch, huh?"

"That's what they say," I said, still smiling. "You don't get it, do you, sweet pea? We do this shit all the time. Whenever one of you muthafuckas messes with the law, they call me down here to straighten you out. Behind the two-way mirror, there's probably a herd of officers jammed in there, just waiting to see what I'm going to do to you."

"You bluffin'."

I walked over to the door and opened it. "See? It's not locked. All you gotta do is find your balls and walk outta here."

"I got balls, bitch," he growled. "And to prove it, I'm gonna fuck you before I leave." Then he tossed the table against the wall like it was a pillow.

"That's the spirit." I smiled, continuing to toss the peach in the air.

He growled and charged at me like a bull, headfirst. I stood in the same spot calmly, waiting until the last possible second, then spun away. He ran headfirst into the wall. Then I tapped on the mirror, signaling them to lock the door. I heard keys jangling just outside the door, then a key entering the lock and the bolt sliding into place.

"Ya hear that?" I asked him. "That's them locking you in."

He shook the cobwebs from his bruised head and stood up. I took a bite from the peach and said, "You all right, sweet pea?"

He charged again, this time using caution. He swung at my head. I moved to the side, just in time. I could feel a breeze go past my head. I took another bite of the peach, which sent him into a rage. He swung again and again, but I remained elusive. He began to perspire profusely. I continued eating.

"When I finish my peach, it'll be my turn. I suggest you do something—quick."

"YOU LITTLE BITCH! I'LL KILL YOU!"

I laughed.

Again, he charged headfirst. And again, I spun out of the way. This time he stopped short of running into the wall. I took the last bite of my peach and threw the pit at him. It hit him in the head.

"You already tried that," I told him, then sucked the residual juice off my fingers. "Well, I'm finished with my peach. Guess I have to get in yo' ass."

"That's how you gon' be sucking my dick when I'm finished with you, bitch!" he screamed. "Just like you suckin' yo' fingers now."

I walked toward him, determined to give him a whipping he wouldn't ever forget. When I was within striking distance, he threw a jab, which I easily deflected, and I continued moving forward. I could see he was about to throw more blows, so I took another step closer, nullifying his long reach. Then I hit him in the forehead with my fist, causing his head to slam against the two-way mirror. I spun around and back fisted him, threw a shot to the groin, another to the throat, an elbow to the jaw, and a powerful palm strike to the sternum. He went down hard. I understood why the police had so much trouble with him when he got back up. Most people wouldn't have been able to withstand a blow like that. The police were overmatched with this man.

I hit him about six more times. His head slammed against the glass with each powerful blow. The punches sounded like hard slaps to the face. He went down again. Having finished him, I turned to leave. Suddenly, he grabbed me around the waist. My back was against his muscular chest. His powerful grip was squeezing the air out of me.

"I GOT YOU NOW, BITCH!"

With lightning speed, I lifted my foot vertically and kicked him in the face, knocking him out cold. I turned around and looked down at the battered prisoner. Then I turned to the two-way mirror, and said, "Make sure you guys charge him with assaulting a federal agent."

CHAPTER 12

CLAYTON POCKETS checked himself and Coco into the Washington Suites hotel in Alexandria. As soon as they entered the room, Coco kicked Clayton in the head with a spinning roundhouse kick, knocking him out. Before he fell, she caught him and lifted him onto her shoulders. She carried him to the bed and removed all of his clothing. Then she tied his hands and feet.

"Clayton. Clayton." She tapped his cheek. "Wake up, sugar."

Slowly, he regained consciousness. When he realized he was tied up, he struggled to free himself.

"What the hell are you doing?" he screamed.

"This is how I like it, sugar," Coco said, cracking her gum. "Never been tied up before, huh?"

"No," he said, calming down. "Why did you have to hit me?"

"Violence makes me horny, sugar," she told him, staying in character. There was no reason to tell him anything before he pleasured her.

"I'm not a prude. All you had to do was ask."

"You might have said no." She smiled and cracked her gum a few more times. "Then I would have wasted my time. And I hate wasting my time. Don't you, Clayton? Like lots of talking when we could be doing it."

Clayton smiled. "Hey, didn't you say something about acupuncture?"

"Yeah. You ready, sugar?"

"Will it hurt?"

"Only if I want it to," she said jokingly, still cracking her gum, "and I don't want it to."

She grabbed a black leather pouch from the nightstand and emptied the contents on his chest. Six vials tumbled out, each containing a long thin needle made of pure gold.

"What are you going to do with those?" he asked nervously. "And why so many?"

"There's only six, sugar."

"Why six?"

"Because six is the number of man. What is a man without his manhood or his ability to reproduce? He ceases to exist. But these six needles, strategically placed, can make a man more virile than he was in his youth."

"But..."

Coco put her fingers over his lips. "Shhhh, no more questions. Try to relax. You're gonna love this." She rubbed her hands on his chest, searching for the right nerve. When she found it, she inserted the first needle. Then she put in four more.

"I don't feel anything."

"You won't until I put this last one in right...here," she said, inserting the final needle.

Suddenly, he felt a powerful erection emerge. "You feel something now?"

"Yeah. What did you do?"

"I increased the blood flow down there by a factor of ten. Can you feel how powerful the throbbing is?"

"Yes."

"And it will stay like that until I remove the needle." She smiled, pulling off her tennis shorts and panties. "You ready, sugar? This is going to be wild."

CHAPTER 13

THE FOUR SEASONS lobby was empty when Kelly and I arrived. The clerk, probably a Georgetown student, was reading a biology book. I flashed my credentials and said, "I'm Special Agent Perry—FBI. This is Agent McPherson. I'm wondering if we could see the phone records for this number."

He looked at the number I gave him. "This number doesn't belong to a specific room. The hotel has lots of numbers like that to accommodate the guests."

"Well, can you print out a list of all the outgoing calls from your guests?"

"Sure, but what's this all about?"

At times like this, when we don't have a warrant, we could play hardball and still not get what we want. Or we could be nice and solicit his help as a patriot. I prefer the latter. The trick is not to lay it on too thick. One time I used the name of a popular president in an attempt to finesse a citizen and found out that he didn't like the guy. I've learned to keep it simple.

"All I can tell you is that this could be very important to a murder investigation."

"Okay, no problem," he said, eager to help. "It'll take a while though." He hit a few buttons on his computer terminal and the printer started. Half an hour later, it stopped. "These are all the calls that went out yesterday."

Kelly and I looked at each other, thinking this was going to take forever. But it was all we had to go on. We sat in Kelly's Stingray trying to decide what would be the best way to tackle this in the least amount of time. I gave her half of the printout, and we started looking for a room from which someone had called the Taylor house. I noticed that the telephone logs were in numerical order by room. They were also logged in time increments. All we had to do was cross-reference the times we'd written down from the caller ID and cell phone.

"I think I got him," I told Kelly after about a half-hour of fruitless searching. "Winston Keyes, room 961. He made four calls to the Taylors."

We went back into the building and asked the clerk if Winston Keyes was still registered.

"No, I checked Mr. Keyes out late Wednesday night."

"Damn!" I said. "Was he alone?"

"Yes."

"Did he have any visitors?"

"That I don't know."

"How did he pay for the room? Did he use a credit card?" I asked, hoping he had so we could track him when he used it again.

"Paid in cash."

"We're going to need to see your security tapes," Kelly said.

CHAPTER 14

COMPLETELY SATISFIED after two hours of nonstop, intense, mind-blowing sex, Coco, still impaled, finally got up. Clayton, lying in the sweat-soaked sheets, had lost track of how many orgasms he'd had, but he wasn't ready to stop.

"What's the matter?" he panted.

"I'm whipped, sugar."

"Just one more," he pleaded, like a crack addict in need of a hit.

"There is one more thing you can help me with, Clayton," Coco said, suddenly serious and no longer speaking with a New York accent. "I need the name of the person who gave you the information on my client."

"What?" He frowned. "What the hell is this? We had a deal!"

"You know, Clayton, acupuncture can cause great pleasure or great pain. It's up to you."

"If I tell you, will you let me go?"

"Sorry, Clayton, no can do. But I promise I'll do it quickly. You won't feel a thing."

Clayton could tell by the look in her eyes that she intended to kill him. He deduced that if the sex she provided was that sensitive and nonstop, the pain she could make him feel would equal the pleasure in intensity.

"Well, if I tell you, will you climb back on me? At least let me go blissfully."

Coco laughed and adopted her New York accent again. "You know, sex would never have been the same after this anyway. The name first.

Otherwise, I'll have to ride you all night. And I just don't have that kinda time, sugar."

"What's to prevent you from killing me as soon as I give you the name?"

"Nothing, sugar. Think about it. I could have tortured the information outta you, couldn'tve I? Instead, I gave you the fuck of your life. I think every man oughta experience this kind of sex at least once in his life."

Although she was smiling, her eyes were cold. Clayton gave her the name of the communications tech and his address. Then Coco climbed on top of him as promised. She waited until he was at the pinnacle of pleasure, then grabbed a hunk of his hair and jerked to the right, snapping his neck. She wiped the room clean, took the sheets and tossed them in a maid's hamper as she left the room and entered an open elevator.

CHAPTER 15

THE VIDEO TECH put the security tape from the lobby of the Four Seasons into the FBI's sophisticated computer. We had to bring the desk clerk with us to identify Winston Keyes, promising him a special tour of FBI Headquarters. The Four Seasons' manager wasn't happy about it, but we needed the clerk.

As far as we knew, the clerk was the only person who could lead us to the killer. I was hoping this wasn't a waste of precious time. It seemed promising, but you never know about leads. I'd wasted lots of time following leads that led to dead ends before. Every law enforcement officer has. But I had a hunch we were on the right track.

The tape was time-date indexed. All we had to do was speed the tape up to the time when Winston Keyes had checked in. The tech froze the picture when the Four Seasons desk clerk identified Keyes, who was looking directly into the camera. The tech hit a couple of buttons, and voila, we had a picture of the man we hoped was our suspect. Keyes was a black man, wearing a chauffeur's uniform. I wondered if Judge Taylor was having an affair with him.

The tech inserted the tape of the floor Keyes was registered for and fast-forwarded. We got lucky again. An expensively dressed white woman was seen entering his suite. She obviously didn't want to be seen. She kept her head lowered, and she was wearing a wide-brimmed sunbonnet.

Either Keyes was having relations with her or he was her driver. Maybe both. I've seen that sort of thing many times. Certainly, someone with more than a chauffeur's pay had to be paying the bill. The Four Seasons was a very expensive hotel. The suite he was staying in was a $5,500-a-night penthouse.

Again we fast-forwarded the tape. At 8:30, Judge Taylor went to the chauffeur's room. According to the time on the tape, the woman who had arrived earlier had been in there with Keyes for six hours. Now Taylor was there, too. Was there some kind of freaky sex going on? I wondered.

Then, unexpectedly, the clerk said, "This may be nothing, but I got a complaint from a guest in the next room about two women arguing. When I called the room, Mr. Keyes apologized and that was the end of it."

Kelly and I looked at each other. We knew we were onto something. What it was, I didn't know yet. We fast-forwarded the tape again and saw Judge Taylor standing in the doorway. It appeared as if she and the other woman were having words. There was a lot of finger pointing from both women.

"Phoenix, what if this is just a guy who got caught screwing around with two wealthy women?" Kelly asked.

"I was wondering about that myself. I'm thinking, this is either the mother lode or this has been a serious waste of time."

The clerk said, "Can I get that tour now, Agent Perry?"

"Sure."

The tech volunteered to show him around. I think she found him attractive. I picked up the telephone logs from Keyes' room, wondering if he had made any other calls in addition to the four to the Taylors. According to the logs, he had made one more call that night. I picked up the nearest phone and punched in the number. A woman's voice informed me that I had reached the Capitol Hill Hyatt Regency. I hung up.

"Hmmmm," I muttered.

"What?" Kelly asked.

"He called the Hyatt Regency right after the Judge left. It may be nothing, but let's check it out anyway. I'm going to take my own car, then go on home. I'm tired."

CHAPTER 16

COCO NIMBURU went to the address that Clayton Pockets had given her. NSA communications tech Gordon Scott lived in a small one-bedroom apartment in Arlington. Using an electronic lock pick, she was able to enter the apartment as if she had the keys. She searched the well-kept premises, thinking this guy must be a real egghead. It was almost 7 p.m. He should be getting home soon, she thought.

Coco sat at the desk in the living room, turned on his Compaq computer, and looked through his files to see if he was a true nerd who brought his work home with him. There was nothing encrypted, nothing suspicious. He probably gave everything to Director Pockets, she deduced. With nothing else to do but wait, she played a few games of solitaire on the Compaq. After losing several games in a row, she was ready to assassinate the computer. She heard keys jangle, then enter the lock on the front door.

She reached for her silenced Makarov as she went toward the door. Gordon Scott walked in, oblivious to her presence. She hit him in the back of the head with the butt of the gun, and he crumpled to the floor. When he woke, he was nude and tied hand and foot to the bedpost with a gag in his mouth. Coco had gotten a chair from the kitchen table and an apple from the refrigerator. When he heard her take a bite, Gordon whipped his head toward her with terror in his eyes. His breathing became heavy, and his chest moved up and down rapidly. He was trying to say something, but the gag muffled his words.

"I know, I know." Coco laughed. "You work hard all day and come home to a bitch like me. Worse than a wife, huh?"

She took a few more bites of the apple, looking into his eyes the entire time. "Ummm, this is so good. You really must tell me where you purchased these."

Gordon frowned, confused as to what she wanted. It certainly couldn't be fruit that could be bought at any grocery store. He searched his mind, trying to figure out what he had done to deserve this. Coco finished the apple, eating the core and seeds as well. Then she wiped her mouth and hands on a paper towel and put it in her pocket.

"I'm an honest woman," Coco began, "so I'm going to tell you the truth. You're going to die today."

Gordon's eyes looked as if they were about to bulge out of his head. He struggled to free himself and appeared to be even more frightened than before.

"You wanna know what you did, right?" Coco asked, completely calm. "You wanna know why, right?"

He nodded as tears crept down his cheeks.

"Somehow, Clayton Pockets found out you were using your position as an NSA communications tech to gather information on people, didn't he?"

Gordon nodded.

"You sold some very sensitive information to Sydney Drew, didn't you?"

He nodded again.

"Did you sell it to anyone else?"

He shook his head.

"Unfortunately, I can't take your word for it. I'm gonna have to make sure." She opened her leather pouch and emptied the vials out onto his chest.

"Are you familiar with acupuncture?"

He shook his head.

"Well, you're about to become acquainted with it. It's going to hurt like hell, but I promise to give you the fuck of your life before you die, okay? It's the least I can do."

CHAPTER 17

THE HYATT REGENCY desk clerk was nothing like our friend from the Four Seasons. She was a first-year Georgetown law student and wanted a warrant for everything. With the flimsy evidence we had, there was no way a judge was going to give us one. I had to go to plan B. I told the clerk that she was obstructing a federal investigation and if she didn't cooperate, I would have her locked up. That got her attention. She was very friendly after that.

I hated roast-beefing citizens. The term stemmed from a legend that had floated around the bureau for years: A New York agent allegedly went to a deli and felt he didn't get enough roast beef on his sandwich so he stood up and said, "I'm FBI!"

The clerk gave us a printout of all the incoming calls to the hotel. We got another phone book of calls. Unfortunately, incoming calls were not logged the way outgoing calls were. Since the hotel doesn't charge the guest for incoming calls, they weren't neatly arranged. I rolled my eyes at the clerk. She smiled triumphantly. I guess she wasn't that scared after all.

That happens sometimes when you roast-beef John Q. Public. They don't cooperate. But I felt it was necessary to get the information. Kelly and I decided to call it a day before tackling the logs. We convinced ourselves that it was probably not going to produce anything anyway. The truth was, I was dog-tired from two hours of sleep, and I wanted to see Keyth and Savannah before I crashed for the night.

When I got home, Savannah greeted me. She was wearing her Mickey Mouse pajamas. She and Keyth were a blessing—my reality check. Nothing is more important than my family—nothing. Some agents are so caught up in the job that they forget they have a life. That's one reason I never went undercover. That's a lonely and dangerous life—especially for a female agent. The entanglements with criminals can get very complicated. And the OPR (Office of Personal Responsibility), the bureau watchdogs, will go after agents if it appears that they are doing something wrong. I guess that's good in a way, but it doesn't do anything for morale.

"Hi, honey." My daughter suddenly energized me. I knelt, and we hugged each other.

"I missed you, Mommy."

"And I missed you, too." I kissed her plump cheek. "Did Daddy feed you?"

"Uh-huh. And it was good, too."

"What did you have?"

"Some mashed potatoes, cream corn, chicken, string beans, rolls, and some Hawaiian Punch."

"Any left?"

"Yeah, Daddy let me fix your plate for you. It's in the microwave. I even set the timer. All you gotta do is push start."

"Hi, baby," I heard my husband say. "How was work?"

"Fine."

Keyth and I discussed cases, but not often. I didn't want my daughter to hear about the gore of the day. I tucked my precious bundle of joy in, and we said our prayers. I kissed her goodnight and went to the kitchen to start the microwave. Keyth was in our bedroom, so I walked in there and collapsed on the bed. We talked for a while, but I have no idea what we talked about. The timer on the microwave went off, and Keyth left to get my plate. By the time he returned, I was out.

CHAPTER 18

WHITE HOUSE CHIEF OF SECURITY Joe Rider had just finished a long, exhausting day, making sure the place where the President slept was safe. Being vigilant for such a long period of time can be draining. It was time to go home, where he could finally drop his guard, if only for the hours he slept. Tomorrow, he would have to be alert, ready for anything. There had never been a penetration at the White House, and if Joe Rider had anything to do with it, there wouldn't be one on his watch either.

Joe Rider had been divorced three times, and his latest girlfriend had left him for a bodybuilder she had met at the gym. All Joe had was the job at which he excelled. He never heard from the three children he had fathered, but that was because he had never put in the time with them when they were young. He was always on special assignment. But that didn't mean he didn't love his wife or his children.

Joe Rider had a tremendous sense of duty, one of many attributes he had acquired from the Marine Corps. He had joined the Corps right after college and had served all over the world. He was a boxer and had won the Marine Corps title. After leaving the Corps, he had become a Secret Service Agent and had worked his way up to White House Security Chief.

Like most people after a long day of work, he wanted to eat and then he wanted to relax in his big leather easy chair that seemed to hug him. Joe had his heart set on the pork chops he'd thought about on and off all day.

He could almost taste the succulent white meat. His plan was to open a bottle of Gewurztraminer, a German-grown, sweet-tasting white wine to enjoy with his meal, then watch a movie and perhaps fall asleep in his comfortable La-Z-Boy. Unfortunately, the Rapist had chosen Joe Rider as his next victim.

The Rapist's lust for violence before ravaging his prey had increased with each new victim. At some point, the violence before the act had become an essential component of the crime. He needed more resistance from the victims to arrive at the level of satisfaction he'd achieved with the first couple that he had attacked. During his two-year reign of terror, he had learned that the men fought harder and longer if he pretended to want their wives or girlfriends.

Then it occurred to him to go after men with power. At first, he went after wealthy men and then big tough-looking men, the kind who went to the gym regularly. Their ability to resist longer stimulated him. Now he wanted Joe Rider. He had to be a tough guy if he protected the President.

The Rapist was already in the house, waiting for Joe to come home. He had followed him for several days and knew his routine. His heart pounded in anticipation when he heard the car pull into the attached garage. It was just a matter of time before Joe walked into the surprise of his life. The door from the garage opened into the kitchen. The Rapist heard Joe toss his keys on the counter.

His footsteps on the hardwood floors told the Rapist exactly where Joe was. He went to the bathroom. The Rapist could hear the flow of urine splashing, then the toilet flushing. The anticipation was almost overwhelming. He hoped Joe would fight long and hard. The bathroom door opened, and he came out. Rider's shocked look when he saw the Rapist was exhilarating. He pointed a gun at Joe's head.

"Let's see your weapon." Joe opened his jacket. "Now, with your left hand, remove it."

Joe followed his instructions, still shocked. He knew he wasn't going to be killed. If the intruder had wanted that, he would have done it already.

"Remove the clip, and dislodge the chambered shell."

Joe followed his instructions to the letter. He began to feel a little more at ease with the situation, and wanted the chance to take on the guy who was brazen enough to enter the home of the Chief of Security. The intruder wanted something, and as far as Joe was concerned, that gave him a distinct advantage.

"Now, drop the gun."

Joe did so.

The Rapist took his eyes off Joe and reached down for the gun. As he knew he would, Joe attacked him and was able to get the gun away from him. He pointed the weapon at the Rapist and pulled the trigger. CLICK, CLICK, CLICK. The gun was empty. A twisted smile emerged on the Rapist's face; then Joe attacked him ferociously with vicious hooks and crosses that would have knocked out Mike Tyson. But the blows didn't faze the Rapist. He was enjoying the punishment.

The Rapist bled easily enough, but there was no stopping him. He was like Joe Frazier fighting Muhammad Ali in their 1972 epic bout in Madison Square Garden. The Rapist could sense that Joe was getting tired. His blows didn't have the same snap and power they'd had earlier in the fight. Besides, they only seemed to make the Rapist stronger.

Joe's face was full of welts and swelling. It wasn't a one-sided fight. The Rapist ran at Joe, tackled him, and punched him in the face until he had no more fight left. Having subdued him, he stripped off his pants.

"NO! DON'T!" Joe screamed when he realized what was going on. But his pleading only added to the Rapist's pleasure.

When the Rapist finished, he left the house. Joe was on the floor, whimpering like a wounded animal. Somehow, Joe found the strength to crawl to his gun. He put the clip back in and chambered a bullet. Then he put the weapon in his mouth and fired.

CHAPTER 19

THE BODY OF CLAYTON POCKETS was found early Saturday morning at the Washington Suites Hotel by a maid who had entered the room when no one answered. She ran out of the room screaming. The local police department was handling the case until they discovered who the victim was. Pockets had registered under a phony name, but it didn't take long for the police to uncover his true identity.

I was on my way to the bureau when Assistant Director Michelson called me on my cell. By the time I got there, there was another mob scene, much like the one at the Taylor house. This time, there were even more satellites and more reporters, which meant more bullshit for the public to sift through. I saw Kelly's Stingray so I knew she was going to bust my chops for not arriving sooner. The murder of NSA Director Pockets was going to mean a tremendous amount of pressure to catch the killer.

According to Michelson, Clayton Pockets was killed the same way Judge Taylor was killed. The only good thing about that information was that we now knew Jennifer Taylor, not her husband, had indeed been the target. It also meant that I didn't have to waste valuable time interviewing feminist leader Patricia English.

I walked into the hotel room and saw Pockets lying nude on the bed, his hands and feet tied to the bedposts. Agents and police officers alike were joking about how he had died. Pockets' balls were purple from repeated orgasms. One officer joked, "If you gotta go, that's the way." Another joked about wanting to be next on her list. No one seemed to be surprised or even interested in the fact that the Assassin appeared to be a woman.

I examined the body more closely and saw the needle pattern in the victim's chest. I recognized it from the time I had spent in the Shaolin Temple. It was the fertility pattern, designed to help a man with a low sperm count continue relations so that a significant amount of semen could be ejaculated. One of the side effects of this sort of acupuncture was that the man wouldn't be able to have sex again for a least a month, maybe six, depending on the man.

The pattern told me that the assailant was familiar with the ancient art. That, coupled with the skill it took to snap a neck so cleanly, led me to believe that the assassin was a martial artist. If I was right, it was going to be tough to catch her. Michelson's cell rang. From the look on his face, it wasn't good news.

"Perry," Michelson said. "We got another stiff. Same MO as Taylor and Pockets. You and McPherson get over there before the media finds out we've got a serial killer out there."

CHAPTER 20

NSA RECEPTIONIST Anita Price told us that Pockets had called in Friday afternoon and said he was taking the rest of the day off, which meant nothing. When she told us he had called from the Capitol Hill Hyatt Regency, I knew we had missed something last night. Nevertheless, we still didn't have enough to get a search warrant. Even if we had a warrant, I had no idea who or what we were looking for.

I looked through the telephone logs the reluctant desk clerk had given us and couldn't make much sense of them, so I decided to do some old-fashioned police work. That meant going to the Hyatt Regency and questioning all the employees.

Director Pockets had called from a pay phone in the lounge. The bartender told us that Pockets had been there, but left with a blonde. He was reasonably confident that he could identify her. We confiscated the security tapes and took the bartender with us to the Hoover Building. With his help, we obtained a picture of the woman Pockets had left with. On the chance that she may have been a guest at the hotel, we put in several other tapes and spotted her coming out of a room on the ninth floor.

From the angle of the videotape, I could see that the room was the last one on the left, next to the exit stairs. We went back to the hotel and called the room to see if she was in. There was no answer. Kelly stayed in the lobby. She was supposed to call me on my cell if the suspect entered the hotel.

I showed the maid my credentials and had her open the door. Careful not to disturb anything, I searched the room and found an electronically locked suitcase. It had a sophisticated ten-button keypad. There could be no doubt now. The blonde was the assassin.

There was a laptop on the dresser, next to the television. I turned it on and searched through the documents. When I saw a file titled "The List," I opened it and saw a list of names. There were addresses and bios next to each name. Judge Taylor was at the top of the list. Suddenly, my cell rang.

"Yeah."

"She's on the elevator," Kelly told me. "Get outta there!"

"You were supposed to tell me when she entered the building."

"A couple of tour buses full of people came in. She must have come in with them. By the time I spotted her, she was on the elevator."

Scrolling down, I saw two names with addresses in San Francisco. I didn't have time to look at every name so I hit the end button to see how long the list was. There were 39 pages of the document. I didn't want to press my luck any further, so I turned off the laptop and ran to the stairs. I heard the elevator bell ping just before I opened the exit door.

CHAPTER 21

THE LAPTOP was still out on the dresser, right where she had left it. Coco couldn't believe she had been so careless, but the chance of someone other than the maid coming into the room was slim. As far as she was concerned, the police were lazy and missed too many opportunities to catch ordinary criminals. They certainly were no match for her, she thought.

Nevertheless, it paid to be careful. She hit the appropriate keys on the suitcase, which contained all sorts of electronic equipment and several other expensive Hollywood-type disguises. She picked up a counter-surveillance device and swept the room for hidden microphones. Nothing registered. A little more relaxed, she turned on the laptop.

Her heart thumped like a sledgehammer when she saw that someone had accessed the hit list files a few minutes ago. Not only had she left the laptop out, she had neglected to lock the files.

The police are not as lazy as I thought. But why didn't they confiscate the laptop and suitcase? Why no microphones? Ahhhh! They didn't have a warrant! That's why! They must still be in the building, probably trying to get one now. Perhaps right outside my door.

She went to the door and listened. Hearing nothing, she looked through the peephole. No one was there as far as she could see, but it was better to be safe than sorry.

Her heart rate slowed. She had a backup plan. But she knew she had to lead her pursuers away from the hotel and then come back later without the De Matteo mask. It was a bold move, but if Coco was anything, she was bold. To be safe, she deleted the hit list file. There would be another laptop and weapons waiting at San Francisco International Airport if she had to leave Washington tonight.

If the police had been in her room, they didn't have time to take down all the names, she thought. To continue working down the list would be difficult for her now, but not impossible. Sydney Drew had to be eliminated tonight, no matter what. Relishing the challenge, she grabbed her suitcase, looked through the peephole once more and left the room.

The plan was to take the suitcase up to the twentieth floor, where she kept a second room—just in case. She always registered under two or three names, paying in advance with a money order. Rarely did she ever need to go to the second room, but it was necessary now. Once in the room, she opened the suitcase and took out an Uzi and several clips. She then took the stairs to the lobby.

When she cracked the door to see if the police were there, she saw Special Agent Phoenix Perry standing by the elevators. She remembered seeing her on television when the president was holding his press conference.

Several tour groups were coming into the lobby. It was now or never. One tour group was about to get on the elevator when Coco opened the stairway door. A woman saw the Uzi and screamed. Phoenix and Kelly turned around and saw the Assassin. They pulled their 9-millimeters out, but people began to scatter in front of them.

Coco seized the opportunity and ran out a door that led to the parking lot. Phoenix and Kelly had to fight their way through the massive crowd, and by the time they got to the parking lot, Coco was on her ninja. She burned rubber and zoomed past them with the front wheel in the air. Barely able to get out of her way, the two agents ran to Kelly's Stingray.

CHAPTER 22

ELLY THREW THE STINGRAY into first gear. The tires spun as we shot out of the parking lot. Tupac Shakur's "Heartz of Men" blared. I turned the stereo off. The suspect was about a block ahead of us. Kelly was going 110 mph, yet the suspect was pulling away. She had to be going over 150 mph. The traffic was starting to get in the way of the chase. Riding a motorcycle enabled the suspect to ride between stopped cars, only inches from disaster, where a car could not follow.

Kelly crossed the yellow lines to gain ground, then crossed back over, escaping a collision with an eighteen-wheeler by the narrowest of margins. I looked at her, aghast at how she was driving. She was oblivious to my daunting stare. Traffic ahead was beginning to back up, but it didn't slow down the suspect. She also crossed the yellow lines and sped up. It looked as if she was going to get away, but Kelly crossed over into the other lane, too. The light was red up ahead. We had her. The suspect had to slow down because of the heavy traffic, I thought, but she didn't. She went right through the light on her back wheel without hesitation.

The crossing traffic put on brakes; tires screeched. Several cars spun out of control into the intersection. We heard metal colliding and glass shattering. Kelly slammed on the brakes, but we just slid, fishtailing out of control. My heart was in my throat. I thought we were going to buy it when I saw two cars coming at my side of the Stingray. They couldn't stop either. I could see the terror on the faces of the drivers. They were that close. Realizing she couldn't stop in time, Kelly took her foot off the brake, shifted gears, and floored it. The two cars just missed us. Up ahead, we saw the suspect heading toward Union Station.

"If she gets to the station, we may never catch her," I said.

"I know, Phoenix. But it's rush hour. The traffic will slow her down. Don't worry. She won't get away."

Soon, we could see her again. We were going to catch her. She was only a few blocks ahead, and the traffic was jammed. I looked at the speedometer. We were going 100 mph. The Assassin looked back and saw us right on her tail. She took off again. What was she doing? I wondered. She was almost at Union Station when a car slammed on the brakes. The motorcycle exploded on impact, throwing the suspect fifty feet ahead of the car she had run into. Somehow, she was able to maintain her balance in the air. Curling into a tight ball, she somersaulted several times and landed on her feet in full stride.

Kelly slammed on the brakes again. We looked at each other, shocked at what we'd just witnessed. The suspect ran into Union Station with Kelly and me hot on her trail. We blasted through the doors at full speed, but she was gone. I was breathing heavily; so was Kelly. I went to the right, Kelly to the left. I bumped into a good-looking, dark-haired woman and excused myself. "Sorry, ma'am." I gasped for air, looking around the station. "FBI. Did a blonde just run past you?"

"Oui. Uh, yes, yes," she told me politely, with a French accent.

"Which way did she go?" I asked, pulling out my weapon. She pointed to the east. I spotted her. She was about to get on the train for New York. "Kelly! This way! I see her."

We hustled over to the woman and yelled, "FBI! FREEZE!" The woman put her hands in the air.

"Me?" she said, still facing the train. "What did I do?"

I jerked her around to face me. It wasn't the woman we suspected. From the back, it had looked like her. "Did you see a blonde run this way?" I asked desperately.

"Yeah. One just ran into the restroom. She may still be in there."

Kelly ran to the restroom, weapon drawn. I apologized to the woman that I had mistaken for the suspect. Surprisingly, she was polite considering the way I had roughed her up and made her miss the train. A moment later, Kelly came out with a sophisticated mask that looked like the woman we had seen on videotape and a frightened woman who said that a woman had knocked her out and taken her clothing. Kelly and I looked at each other, shaking our heads. We knew Michelson was going to go nuts over this. He might have forgiven the high-speed chase and endangering innocent citizens if we had caught her. But since we hadn't, we were in trouble—big-time.

CHAPTER 23

I

T WAS PERSONAL NOW. For the first time, someone had scared Coco Nimburu. The danger excited her. She had just had an encounter with an agent who had chased and almost killed her. She could tell from the look in her eyes that Phoenix Perry was determined to catch her. If necessary, she would scour the entire station, looking for the smallest clue to her whereabouts.

The other agent seemed to be equally determined, driving at speeds exceeding 100 mph with little regard for civilians. These two were good and relentless. Were it not for her own great athletic ability and martial arts skills, Coco would surely be dead or in chains.

She casually walked up the stairs to the street and flagged a cab. On the way back to the Capitol Hill Hyatt Regency, she began to plot the demise of her new archenemy. First, she was going to find out absolutely everything there was to know about Phoenix Perry. The cab stopped in front of the hotel, which was inundated with cops. But they had no idea what Coco really looked like. So they checked her ID, which was flawless, and then made sure she was a registered guest and let her by.

Coco returned to her twentieth-floor room and disrobed, leaving each garment on the floor where it dropped. Still hyped from the chase, she needed a hot bath and sex, both of which would be taken care of in the bathtub. Climbing into the tub, she positioned herself under the faucet so that she could feel the nonstop splash of warm water on her sensitive clitoris. She laid back and let the water run for about an hour, then bathed.

CHAPTER 24

T HE BUREAU had an unwritten rule. To err is human; to forgive is not FBI policy. It's funny, right up until the moment you find yourself getting your ass chewed like there's no tomorrow. On our way back to the hotel, Kelly and I drove past the accident that had resulted from our high-speed chase. There were five EMS vehicles on the scene.

I saw Michelson when we pulled into the Capitol Hill Hyatt Regency parking lot. He didn't look happy. Kelly got out of the Stingray and waited for me. I was thinking about the Assassin.

"I'm glad you're runnin' the show on this one, Phoenix," Kelly joked, checking her precious Corvette for any scratches. "Nothing happened to my baby. So life is good."

I couldn't help laughing. I loved her sense of humor. She had a way of making the direst situation less dreadful.

"We're in trouble, Kelly. The woman we chased is a highly skilled martial artist, probably trained all her life. She's powerful, balanced, and keeps her head in the heat of battle. She won't be taken alive."

"Yeah, and she's also a nymphomaniac." Kelly smiled.

I grinned. "Seriously, Kelly. When we find her again, I want you to stick close to me. You don't have the training to go at her one on one. I'm not sure I have the training either."

We had started for the hotel lobby when Michelson stormed around the corner. Always well-groomed, Michelson was a spit-and-polished FBI man. His personal motto was "Never make the bureau look bad." Michelson had a way of making you feel like a complete buffoon without saying a word. The look on his face was sufficient, and I would have settled for the stare rather than being blasted by his harsh words.

"All right! You two have had enough time to get your stories together!" he shouted. "What the fuck happened, Perry?"

"Could you, like, lower the volume?" Kelly asked.

"SHUT UP, MCPHERSON!" Michelson yelled. "Keep that up, and you'll be on suspension so long, you'll forget you were ever an agent." He was still staring at Kelly when he screamed, "I'm waiting, Perry!"

"Well, sir," I began, knowing I was already on thin ice, "we came here on a slim lead. After the bartender identified the woman Director Pockets had left the lounge with, we were going to go to her room and ask her some questions. Then she took off. We didn't want to lose her."

"But you lost her anyway, didn't you?" He glared at me. "How did she know you were after her specifically? HUH? You went into her room without a warrant, didn't you? She realized it and made a run for it, didn't she?"

I remained silent.

"How many times have we trained for this? HOW MANY? Agent Perry, we train for this to make sure that when we take a suspect down, we take him down right. That means no innocent civilians get hurt, isn't that right?"

"Yes, sir."

"But you two hot dogs had to do it on your own and now we've got a fuckin' circus. And to top that shit off, you've made the President look like a goddamned idiot. He's the one who vouched for you on national television. Now look at this shit! We've got a seven-car pileup, eight civilians with major injuries being rushed to the hospital, and nobody in custody."

I remained quiet, taking my tongue lashing like a good little girl. Sometimes I hated being an FBI agent; this was one of them.

"Well, what do you have to say for yourself, Perry?"

"Sir, we learned that she's an incredible martial artist. Probably one of the best in the world, judging by her incredible balance and her ability to keep a cool head in a frantic situation. Also, she's a master of disguise. I think she's Kunoichi—female ninja. And if I'm right, we're going to need a lot more people on this."

"Is that what you want me to tell the director?" Michelson growled. "You want me to tell him we're after a female ninja who can look like anyone?"

"Don't forget to tell him she's also a nymphomaniac," Kelly said, interjecting her biting sarcasm. "I'm sure St. Clair would want to know that, too."

"NOT ANOTHER FUCKIN' WORD, MCPHERSON!" Michelson snapped. "You two get the hell outta here. You're off the case. In fact, you're on suspension until further notice. Ford and Flynn are taking over."

CHAPTER 25

ROOM 1619 was being meticulously examined by the forensics team when Michelson returned. He called Ford and Flynn outside and told them they were in charge of the case, strongly admonishing them not to blow it. Eager to get a chance to atone for past screw-ups, they thanked him for the opportunity.

As they walked with him to the elevator, Michelson briefed them on the case and told them to talk to Agent Perry to get the rest of the information; then he got into the elevator. He waited until the two agents turned away before he pushed the button for the twentieth floor.

Coco Nimburu opened the door when she saw Michelson through the peephole. They embraced and kissed passionately. She pulled off her robe and exposed her nakedness to him, then tore at his clothes like a ravenous wolf. Coco liked Michelson, but she knew that one day she would have to kill him, too. He knew what she looked like without the disguises.

They were employed by the same client and had been paid handsomely for their part in the killings several months earlier. Michelson was on the inside, gathering information on all the people on Coco's hit list. Their relationship had started out professionally but had become sexual almost immediately.

Now they were grunting and groaning like wild animals in heat. Michelson was the one man who could keep up with Coco without the aid of acupuncture. It was going to be a shame to kill him, but she always had the needles.

After a couple of rounds of satisfying sex, Michelson said, "I took her off the case, Coco. You oughta be able to finish up in Washington and maybe San Francisco before St. Clair puts her back on the case. Ford and Flynn won't give you any trouble. Both of them are serious fuck-ups."

"I want Perry on the case, Lawrence. Put her back on."

"Why?"

"Because she's a worthy opponent. I want the challenge of her trying to stop me from carrying out my assignment."

"Is that wise? Why even risk it?"

"Because she scares me, and I like it."

"Well, it's outta my hands. The suspension came straight from the top. Nothing I can do about it, either."

"I'll take care of it," Coco said. "Did you bring me the info on Perry and the blonde?"

"Yes, it's in my briefcase. I'll get it for you." As he walked across the room, Michelson remembered the conversation with agent Perry in the parking lot. "By the way, she knows you're Kunoichi."

"Ah, a worthy opponent indeed. I'm going to enjoy turning her life upside-down."

Michelson came back to the bed with the files on the two agents and handed them to her. Then he went into the bathroom to take a shower. Coco opened Perry's file first. She discovered that Sydney Drew was her father, and it brought a smile to her face. She learned that Phoenix had spent twelve years in a Shaolin Temple honing her skills in Kung Fu. Her mother had died giving birth to her, which is why she was named Phoenix. Her name would symbolize the death and rebirth of her mother for as long as she lived.

CHAPTER 26

THE EVENING NEWS did a hatchet job on Kelly and me. Keyth and I sat on the couch, watching, shaking our heads as they distorted everything. They chronicled the investigation and made me look like a Keystone cop. Somehow they found out that Director Pockets was deeply in debt and hinted that he was taking bribes for investigating private citizens.

He had used Gordon Scott to tap telephones and dig into all sorts of personal information on selected people so Clayton Pockets could black-mail them. What I found particularly deplorable was how they connected the murder of Judge Taylor to these two sleazeballs by simply asking, "What did Clayton Pockets have on Supreme Court nominee Jennifer Taylor?"

"See, baby," Keyth began, "that's why you need to leave the bureau and come into business with me and your father. Those bastards don't care about how that question sullies her reputation. If she weren't a conserva-tive, do you think they would say some shit like that? HELL NO! I guess what's pissing me off even more is the fact that none of the black organizations are standing up for her. And I bet that witch Patricia English is loving this electronic lynching."

"I know, Keyth, I know."

"Let's take advantage of your suspension and take a mini-vacation. I'm thinkin' maybe a trip to St. Thomas. We could leave tonight. My mother could take care of Savannah while we take moonlight walks on the sand, sip margaritas, and make love all night long."

"Sounds good to me. Call your mother, and I'll let Savannah know we're leaving for the weekend."

"I'll call your dad first and let him know."

"Have you and Dad discussed the murders?"

"To tell you the truth, no, we haven't. We've been so busy at the office that we haven't discussed anything but our own cases. I don't think Sydney knows anything about Pockets' murder. If he does, he hasn't said anything to me about it."

CHAPTER 27

SYDNEY DREW listened to his son-in-law's voice on the answering machine at gunpoint. Coco Nimburu was listening, too. Now that she knew Agent Perry was leaving town, she decided to have a couple of surprises ready for her when she returned from her romantic excursion. Keyth Perry sounded excited about going to St. Thomas. Coco grinned fiendishly. The plan she had for Agent Perry only added to her licentious state of mind.

With a libido like Coco's, just about anything caused her lascivious juices to flow. That's one reason she always took her golden needles with her to every kill. The needles served two purposes. If a man was the target, she could satisfy her own lust and then convince herself that she was sending him to his maker blissfully. If the target was a woman, the needles could be used as a means of torture.

As an afterthought, Keyth Perry mentioned the murders of Clayton Pockets and Gordon Scott. Sydney Drew was unaware of their deaths, but now he understood what was going on and why this woman was holding a gun on him. He had just arrived home from an eighteen-hour workday after stopping by Mister Big Stuff's World Famous Barbecue restaurant to pick up some of their famous ribs.

He had requested extra sauce for the ribs and could hardly wait to get home to devour them. Now he was looking down the barrel of a silenced Makarov, and his appetite had disappeared. He knew why the woman was there and who had sent her. Ironically, the same person who was paying her to kill him had also been instrumental in helping him get his investigative firm up and running.

Coco felt sorry for Sydney, but her feelings wouldn't stop her from killing him. According to his dossier, he had forty years of government service, twenty as a naval intelligence officer and twenty with the National Security Agency. After the death of his wife, he had thrown himself into his work and caring for his daughter. They were inseparable.

When relatives offered to keep Phoenix while he traveled the world eavesdropping on foreign powers, he declined their generous offers, preferring to have her with him. He was a true patriot and believed that his work was important to America's survival. His views on patriotism were passed on to Phoenix, which was one reason why she had become an FBI agent.

"You mind if I sit down?" Sydney asked politely. "It's been a long day and this is a perfect ending to it."

Curious, Coco frowned, wondering why he wasn't begging for his life or even asking her why she was doing this. She gestured with the pistol. Sydney grunted a little as he sat down. He chuckled and said, "My grandmother once told me that when you start to grunt when you sit down or before you get up, that's when you know you're getting old."

Coco smiled. It was an amusing story but held some truth. For the first time since Sydney had walked in, she really looked at him. She could see Phoenix in his face. The resemblance evoked questions about her in Coco's mind.

"I'm an honest woman, Sydney. I'm going to kill you tonight. Nothing can change that. But how you die, how painful it is, well, that depends on you. If you answer some questions, I'll send you out of this world with pleasure you won't believe. It's up to you."

Coco was a beautiful woman, but her penetrating eyes and the confidence with which she spoke made Sydney take her threats seriously.

"What do you want to know?"

"When most people see me in their homes, they become so frightened that they begin to beg for their lives, or they offer me bribes. But you, you just accepted your fate like a samurai. Why?"

"Because, deep down, I always knew you would show up, and I know who's paying you. The person also gave me the startup money for my business and sent me clients to keep it going. Because of your client, I've made honest money doing the same thing I did for the government for far less money than what I've pulled in the last year or so."

"So you knew it would come to this?"

"I suspected it. But it was too good a deal to pass up. I was retired with almost nothing to show for forty years of government service. I trained Gordon Scott to take over my job when I left. He supplied me with some information about your client, which is why you killed him, I suspect." She nodded. "Why Clayton Pockets? Not that I liked the SOB."

"He was blackmailing my client. He loved the ponies just a little too much. He was on the verge of losing everything. I can understand his desperation. But as they say, if you dance to the music, you gotta pay the piper."

"So your client was planning to kill me all along because of what I knew?"

"Probably. I don't know. But, considering what you just told me, that would be my guess."

Sydney Drew shook his head and muttered, "That's ruthless as hell."

"May I ask you about your daughter?"

"What does my daughter have to do with this?" Sydney asked, suddenly fearful for Phoenix's safety. "You're not going to kill her, are you?" Coco was quiet. "You said you were an honest woman. Tell me the truth. Are you going to kill my daughter?"

"Only if I have to. She chased me through the streets of Washington with a relentlessness that matched my own. She isn't the type to give up once she sets her mind to something, is she?"

"No, she isn't. Please don't kill my daughter. Please don't kill her. She's all that's left of her mother and me."

"I don't have a contract for her, so if I can avoid it, I will. But if I'm cornered and it's me or her, you will see her sooner than you think." Relief flooded Sydney's face. "Now, tell me. How old was she when the Shaolin monks accepted her?"

"Six."

"I was five when I began my training," Coco said reflectively. "And how long did she train there?"

"Twelve years. Part of the reason I stayed in China as long as I did was so she could continue her training. You always wanna encourage your children when they take the initiative."

"So it was her idea to study the art?"

"Yes. I took her to a Kung Fu demonstration, and it was love at first sight."

"I see. Then you returned to America, and she went on to college. And the rest is, as they say, history." He nodded. "Well, would you like to eat your food?"

"No. I don't have much of an appetite now."

"I understand." Coco smiled. "I'll make sure it doesn't go to waste."

CHAPTER 28

T HE NEW NINJA MOTORCYCLE was just a a half-block away from Sydney
    Drew's home in Takoma Park. If she hurried, she could get to Silver
    Spring, take care of Senator Blevins and her husband, and get back to
the Hyatt Regency before midnight. As she rode the peppy bike to her
next victim's home, Coco thought about the class Sydney Drew had shown
when she had intruded into his home. She liked him, and she would keep
her word not to kill Phoenix unless she had to. But it was still personal. She
could do so many things to Phoenix. Killing her was only one of them.

Killing Drew, Coco knew, would give Phoenix Perry great incentive to
track her down. Sure, Perry had seen the list. She might even have known
the names and addresses of the intended victims, Coco thought, but she
didn't know when and where she would strike next. It could be in San
Francisco, Denver, Chicago, Manhattan, or perhaps Washington, D.C.

Originally, she had planned to start in Washington, head west, and work
her way back to Manhattan. The most important people on the list were in
the D.C. area, where Taylor, Pockets, Scott, Drew, and the Blevins lived.
The rest of the hits could be done at random.

Coco knew that Phoenix would spend every waking hour trying to figure
out what she was going to do next. Phoenix was going to need her help to
keep up with her. Coco decided she would assist her by calling or leaving
clues along the way. It was going to be a blast playing with her and still
getting away with a coast-to-coast murder spree.

The only thing that bothered her was that there weren't many men left on the list to have sexual relations with. Women were fair game, but they didn't have penises; therefore, the needles served no useful purpose. Maybe I'll pick up some strays along the way, Coco thought. A pizza guy, a waiter who delivered room service, a bartender, a desk clerk; there were so many to choose from. The thought of it made her wet.

The client had told her to take out Martha Blevins with extreme prejudice. She didn't know what the problem was between them, but this assassination would be a personal one for the client. The murder of Chester Blevins would be incidental, so she would give him a merciful, blissful sendoff—one that he would enjoy and one that would give Coco pleasure as well. But Martha Blevins would be given no such quarter. Her murder would be quite painful.

When she arrived at the Blevins' house in Silver Spring, Coco parked her bike in the driveway, walked up to the front door like she was a Girl Scout selling cookies, and rang the doorbell. Chester opened the door to the surprise of his life. He was short but handsome with graying temples. Coco put her weapon to his forehead and strode into the house like she owned the place, closing the door behind her. Fear and dread engulfed Chester.

"Martha—where is she?"

"In the kitchen."

"Cooperate and I'll give you pleasure like you've never known. Refuse and die a slow, agonizing death. It's up to you."

Chester nodded his head rapidly as she knew he would. In her years as an assassin, not one man ever chose an agonizing death when he could go out with unbelievable pleasure. She removed the pistol from his forehead and put it under his chin. Then she kissed him deeply, pulling the back of his head forward to meet her lips. After the kiss, she felt his privates to see what he had to offer, not that it mattered. A stiff penis was all she needed.

"Let's go get your wife, Chester."

More obedient than man's best friend, Chester led her down the hallway to the kitchen where Martha was cooking a pot of spaghetti and meatballs. She was facing the stove, but she heard him come in.

"Who was it, Chester?" Martha asked without turning around. "You simply must taste this sauce. It's the best I've ever made." She turned around with a large wooden spoonful of meat sauce in her hand. She dropped the spoon and gasped when she saw Coco Nimburu standing next to Chester with a gun under his chin.

"What's going on?" Martha shouted. "What do you want? Money?"

"No, not money, Martha," Coco said calmly. "I don't want anything from you, but Chester and I just made a deal that will be mutually pleasurable for the both of us. You, on the other hand, will have to wait until we're finished. I'll deal with you then."

Coco thought it best not to tell them that they would both be dead by the time she left. That way, she wouldn't have to hear the constant begging that doomed people did. Plus, if Chester thought by pleasuring Coco, he and Martha might live, it would be easier for him when she sent him to meet his maker.

"What do you think, Chester? Should we make her watch?" He shook his head. "Don't want the old broad to see you getting your freak on, huh? I understand. Let's go, you two."

She tied Martha's hands and feet and put her in their bedroom closet; then she told Chester to strip. Inside the closet, Martha could hear Chester's prurient groans of ecstasy. It went on and on for about an hour. Then she heard what sounded like a twig snapping, followed by a short gag. Wondering what had happened, she tried to listen more closely. The sex was over, that much she could tell. Was Chester all right? She could hear footsteps coming toward the closet. Maybe it was Chester, she thought. Maybe he had some-how freed himself, fooling the intruder into thinking he had enjoyed sex with her. Maybe it was she who had gagged suddenly. The door opened.

"Your turn, Martha." Coco backhanded her. Then she proceeded to beat Martha to a pulp, breaking both her arms and legs before putting a bullet in her brain. As usual, Coco took the sheets and any DNA evidence they held with her. An hour later, she was back in her room on the twentieth floor of the Hyatt Regency, watching *Star Trek Voyager* and eating the ribs she had taken from Sydney Drew's place.

PART 2
LET THE GAMES BEGIN

CHAPTER 29

THE BELTWAY traffic was heavy, and the Rapist was in the fast lane going 40 mph. After driving back and forth for a couple of hours, he was about to call it a night. No one was taking the bait. Instead of flashing their lights, the drivers of the other cars switched lanes and zoomed past him. He was just about to switch lanes to take his exit when a motorist came out of nowhere, flashing his lights and blowing the horn like a maniac. The Rapist smiled broadly and switched lanes. The driver zoomed past in a black Cadillac and shook his fist at him. The Rapist had to speed up so he wouldn't lose the motorist, yet stay far enough behind not to be spotted.

The Rapist followed the Cadillac to Union Station, which not only contained Amtrak's headquarters but also housed the city's most elegant mall, 130 shops and a nine-screen movie complex. The driver parked in the connected garage and practically ran to the escalators, totally unaware he was being followed. The Rapist saw the driver go into Victoria's Secret. He walked past the glass-enclosed shop. His intended victim was talking to a short blonde. Ten minutes later, the driver and the woman came out of the shop holding hands.

The Rapist followed the couple down the spiral staircase, past the bronze statue of A. Philip Randolph, to the huge food court featuring a smorgasbord of food from all over the world. The Rapist watched the couple walk hand in hand over to the Chinese food restaurant, which was next to a New York-style pizza parlor. They ordered shrimp with lobster sauce, beef fried rice, sweet-and-sour shrimp and egg-drop soup to go. The smell of pizza filled the Rapist's nostrils, and he ordered a slice. It tasted so good that he ordered another slice and a root beer to wash it down.

The Rapist took a seat in the food court and scrutinized the couple while he finished his pizza. The man was tall and athletic. He had broad shoulders and a deep, muscular chest. The woman was wearing a low-cut lavender dress that hugged every voluptuous curve.

After about ten minutes, their food was ready, and they strolled out of Union Station with their fingers laced. The woman had her head on the man's shoulder; she felt safe. The couple stopped at Ben and Jerry's and picked up some ice cream. By the time they arrived at a house in Bethesda, it was 10:30.

The Rapist pulled into the driveway and parked right behind them. He flashed his bright lights in their eyes. The man got of out his Cadillac and slammed the door.

"HEY MAN! WHAT THE FUCK!" he shouted.

The Rapist picked up the duct tape on his front seat and got out of the car, brandishing his gun. He said, "How 'bout we go inside, and discuss this in private? Okay, tough guy."

"Hey, what's this about, man?" He changed his tone.

"I said, let's discuss it inside. Now get the bitch and let's go."

The Rapist followed the couple into the house, looking around to see if anybody had seen him. They went to the bedroom, and the man said, "What do you want—money, jewelry, what? We just wanna eat our food, watch a movie, and fuck. I've been waiting all day for this shit, man."

"I'm not a thief," the Rapist said. He tossed the tape on the bed. "Strip, honey."

"So you wanna fuck my bitch? Is that what this is about?"

"Chad! I told you not to call me that!"

"That's all you are. And that's all you're ever gonna be."

The Rapist frowned. This wasn't exactly what he had hoped for. Chad wasn't even in love with the woman. No way he'd fight hard for her. He had to think of something fast. If he left without raping somebody, they wouldn't hesitate to call the police and give them a description. He decided to go through with the charade, thinking maybe when it began, Chad would try to fight.

"Strip, honey," the Rapist repeated.

"CHAD! DO SOMETHING?"

"Yeah, Chad, do something," the Rapist urged.

"You wanna fuck Cindy? Be my guest. It ain't worth gettin' killed over."

"YOU SON-OF-A-BITCH!" Cindy shouted. "Is that all I am to you? Is that all I am?"

"Yeah. What the fuck else? I hope you don't think I'm gonna marry you."

Cindy slapped Chad, and Chad slapped her back. She tried to slap him again, but he grabbed her arm.

"Hey, knock that shit off," the Rapist told them, but they kept wrestling. He didn't want to fire a shot. Someone would hear it and call the police. His instincts told him to leave while he could, but they both had seen his face. He hit Chad in the back of the head with the gun, thinking the blow would knock him out and give him time to think. But Chad turned around and grabbed the gun. While they wrestled for the weapon, Cindy ran to the hallway closet and came back with a Louisville slugger.

Chad was strong, and if the situation had been different, his strength would have given the Rapist a stiff erection. But it was life or death now. The Rapist tried to get the gun away from Chad. Suddenly, he felt a blunt object crash against his back. It hurt like hell, but he couldn't let go of the gun. THUD! Cindy hit him again.

"Let Chad go!" she shouted. The gun was slipping out of the Rapist's hand. THUD! Again, she hit him. POW—the gun went off. The bullet ripped through Chad's chin and out the top of his head.

"Chad?" Cindy uttered, unable to believe what she was seeing.

It had happened so fast. She dropped the bat and ran over to her lover's dead body. The Rapist's mind was racing a hundred miles an hour. For the first time since he had started raping men two years ago, he was scared. Cindy was crying uncontrollably. The Rapist knew he had to kill her. There was no other way. He sighed deeply, then put the gun to her head and fired.

CHAPTER 30

S T. THOMAS was beautiful and a welcome getaway from Washington. Keyth and I had a huge suite that overlooked the white sand beach. We had just made love, and I opened the terrace door to let some fresh air in. A breeze filled the room and dried the sweat on my naked body. Keyth grabbed me around the waist. "Gotcha," he said. I screamed a little when I felt his sudden touch, then laughed. "I love you, baby," he told me.

"I love you, too."

"So what do you wanna do for fun tonight?"

"Oh, I don't know. Maybe dance, or maybe we can stay in the room." I giggled. "Let's see what Kelly and Simon want to do."

"They're probably doing what we just finished doing," Keyth said, nibbling on my ear.

"Probably. Kelly's a real sexpot."

"Like you're not."

We stood at the door of the terrace, our naked bodies glistening as the sun set in the distant sky. The glow of it, the beauty of God's creation, was awesome to behold. I remembered that when I was a child in China with my dad, we'd watch the stars. I tried to count them but never could. The beauty of the midnight sky had fascinated me, as it still does.

The warmth of my husband's touch, a beautiful sunset, and not a care in the world relieved the stress of being Special Agent in Charge Phoenix Perry. But it didn't free my mind of thoughts about the Assassin, whose presence I felt even though she was so far away, still on a killing rampage, I suspected.

I was bothered by my inability to let go of the case, even though I was on a romantic weekend with the love of my life. It felt strange. I was starting to become like so many agents who couldn't separate their personal lives from their jobs. Maybe it was time to leave the bureau.

Maybe I should take my dad up on his offer to come into the business with him. God knows it would be easier on my family, and I'd probably have better hours. I wouldn't have to feel guilty about leaving Savannah all the time and worrying about her while I was on the job.

Losing focus could mean losing your life or causing the death of a partner. The last thing I ever want on my conscience is something happening to Kelly because I was thinking about my family and not staying alert on the job.

I felt Keyth biting into my neck. Not hard, but hard enough to leave evidence that he had been there. I felt myself slipping into the moment and loving it. He turned me around to face him. I could see more than desire in his eyes. Devotion is what registered. At that moment, I was glad that Keyth and I had waited until we got married before we plundered each other's bodies. He's the only man I've ever known, and it made me feel special that he was willing to wait and not pressure me. Although I will admit there were times during heavy petting when, had he not said no, I would have given myself to him.

"Keyth?" He was still biting into my flesh.

"Yeah, baby?" He momentarily released the grip his warm mouth had on my neck.

"Do you remember what you told me when we were at the altar? You know, that list of things you loved about me?"

"Of course, I do."

Playfully, I said, "Prove it."

"What do I get if I do?"

"Anything you want." I smiled.

"Okay, here goes. Phoenix Drew, I believe in you. I trust in you, fully and completely. When I'm with you, I want to wrap myself in your virtue—your honesty. I adore your ability to make the people around you feel special. Thank you for coming into my life." He paused for a second. "Well, did I get it right?"

"Yes, you did. Promise me something, honey."

"Anything."

"Promise me you'll never forget those words, okay? They remind me of what's truly important."

"I won't."

We kissed again, longer and more deeply. My craving for him was renewed with even greater intensity. I ached for Keyth. I felt him against me. But I wanted to kiss him just a little longer—the best foreplay. A sigh escaped my intoxicated mind and found its way out of my open mouth. I was putty in my husband's capable hands—he knew all the right spots. I could hardly stand it.

Then he touched me. The exactness of his touch, the precision of it, the timing was all so perfect—I shivered. He laid me down on the floor, and I surrendered willingly, deliberately. I was losing myself more and more. My mind was somewhere between heaven and earth. The world was still; only Keyth and I existed. Then I opened my eyes and saw the stars beginning to shine in the evening sky. It was the perfect ending to an already incredible day.

CHAPTER 31

H AVING REGAINED CONSCIOUSNESS, we could hear Kelly and Simon next door on the terrace. Kelly was loud, and Simon was yelling, "IS THAT HOW YOU LIKE IT?"

"YES, YES! OH YES!"

Keyth and I laughed. The screaming went back and forth for another five minutes or so; then quiet consumed the night. A few minutes later, Kelly called and asked if we wanted to go down to the hotel-sponsored beach party. I told her we'd meet them in about an hour. Then I showered and perfumed.

We left the suite and went down to the beach, where many of the hotel guests were gathered. The nights were cool, but it was still a little sticky out. I had decided to wear a multicolored bikini with a matching sarong that extended to my ankles.

A Jamaican band was singing Ziggy Marley's version of "No Woman No Cry." They were good. I saw Kelly and Simon at a table near the dance floor. Simon was a tall, well-built white D.C. detective with a pleasant personality. He would go on to become police commissioner someday, I thought. Kelly really cared about him. He was one of several hundred officers in the police department who wanted to date her. But Simon was just smart enough to let Kelly come to him; at least that's his version of the events that brought them together.

"Hi, lovebirds," I said when we reached the table. "I know you two are having a wild time." Kelly smiled when I looked at her. She knew I had heard them on the terrace. I just wanted to bust her chops a little. "So what are you guys having? I'm starved."

"I'll bet you are." Kelly laughed. "Somebody was pretty loud upstairs."

Keyth and Simon were used to our back-and-forth verbal jabs. I loved Kelly, and she loved me. I don't know how we had become so close, but we had clicked almost immediately at Howard University. From the day I had met her, she had just been so down-to-earth.

"Can I get you something to drink, baby?" my husband asked.

"I want some food, Keyth. Bring me a chicken kabob with shrimp."

Simon went off with Keyth to get the food.

CHAPTER 32

I WAS FOCUSED ON the Assassin, going over everything in my mind, trying to figure out what was going on. I had worked with Kelly long enough to know that she was thinking about the case, too.

"So what have you come up with so far, Kelly?"

"I think we've got a homicidal nymphomaniac who, judging by the name she chose to register under, has deep desires to be a Hollywood actress. And if not that, she loves to be on stage. Probably watches the news to see what people are saying about her."

"I agree, and I think if we're going to catch her, we'll have to be on the lookout for Hollywood names. I think she's been using celebrity names for some time now. I don't think she'll change. She's also arrogant. A professional like her would never leave evidence of her crimes out in the open like that."

"You think she'll use that name again?" Kelly asked.

"Hard to say. She may, just to throw us off the trail."

"How so?"

"Well, if she registers as Susan Lucci again, we have to bite on something like that, which would give her more time to do whatever she wants while we waste valuable time staking out a room she has no intention of returning to. On the other hand, she may use it because we would think that she's too smart to try that again. You never know with a cold-blooded killer like her."

Keyth and Simon came back with our food. Then Keyth said, "I know you two are talking about the Assassin, aren't you?"

"Yes, but we're done," I told him.

"No, go ahead. Simon and I wanna watch the De La Hoya fight. The bartender told us they were showing it in the hotel lounge. Do you mind?"

Normally I would watch the fights with my husband, but he was right. I did want to discuss the case with Kelly. "Keyth, tell the truth. If the fight wasn't on, would it be okay if Kelly and I discussed the case?"

He laughed.

"I knew that was only an excuse to watch. Just wanted you to know I wasn't fooled," I told him.

"Okay, you got me. We'll be back when it's over, which could be five minutes or an hour."

"Okay. If we're not here when you guys come back, we'll be upstairs."

After they left, Kelly said, "You two have a great relationship. I admire it. You guys still make passionate love. It's hard to believe you're married to each other."

"Well, when you find the right one, it will be like that," I told her. "You thinkin' about marrying Simon?"

"We've talked about it. He wants to, but I've been down that road before. Besides, Simon has secrets that he's unwilling to share with me. He tells me to be patient and he'll open up, but I don't know. Something kinda bothers me about him. We've been together for a year-and-a-half now and he still hasn't opened up. I haven't even met his parents."

"Really? After a year-and-a-half? Why do you bother? You're not getting any younger," I said.

Kelly grinned. "Because the sex is good. But I'm not sure if he's the one. If I ever get married again, I need my man to be more open. Until that happens, I don't see any reason to rush into anything."

"I know what you mean. Don't do it unless you're sure, Kelly. Don't let him or anyone else pressure you into doing something you'll regret later."

"I won't." She sipped her margarita. "Why do you think she's killing key government officials?"

"It doesn't make much sense. If it were just the NSA Director and the communications tech, that would give us reason to concentrate there. But the judge doesn't fit with those two."

"I know. And what about the people at the Four Seasons? How do they fit into all of this? Or do they? Is it possible that it was just a coincidence that Winston Keyes called the Hyatt Regency?"

"Maybe, but I doubt it. Keyes and the woman probably have a lot to do with it. The problem is, we don't have anything on Keyes and we don't know who the rich woman is. We don't even know if Winston Keyes is his real name. I mean, if the Assassin can register under Susan Lucci, Keyes could certainly be an alias."

"The Assassin has the advantage. She knows where, when, and who the next targets are—if there are any more targets. She's run up a serious total as it is."

"They'll be more, Kelly. I saw part of the list, remember? Besides, if there weren't any more, why was she still at the hotel after she hit Gordon Scott? She should've been gone long before we got to the hotel, don't you think?"

"Good point. Okay, then we need to start checking other hotels. But then, that would be like searching for a needle in a haystack. She could be anywhere, from D.C. to Alexandria to Bethesda and anywhere in between."

"Maybe. Or maybe she's bold enough to stay in D.C. I mean, she picked a hotel a few blocks away from FBI headquarters, for God's sake. If she would do that, she's bold enough to pick a hotel right in the heart of D.C., maybe even the same hotel."

Kelly and I looked at each other. We were thinking the same thing.

"That would be perfect," I continued. "Who would think to look in the same hotel for a fleeing assassin? Come to think of it, when I briefed Ford and Flynn, I asked them about the suitcase and laptop. They said they didn't find either."

"Maybe she hid them somewhere in the hotel and came back to get them."

"No, she had another room, Kelly. No way she would just leave them hidden somewhere for the FBI to find. She had another room. That's where she put them. Then led us away from the hotel. I bet she went right back after she ditched us."

"Exactly. She had gotten rid of the disguise. She could waltz right back in there, and no one would suspect her. We gotta tell Ford and Flynn. They can view the videotapes. Maybe they'll spot her. And if we're truly lucky, she'll still be there."

"Why wouldn't she be? She thinks she's so much smarter than us."

"Well, she is pretty damn smart, Phoenix."

"I know; I just don't want to admit it." I laughed.

"What do we do if she's not there?"

"Then we concentrate on the judge. We find out who had a grudge against the judge and who had the money to pay an expensive girl like Susan Lucci." It was the only name we had for her. Might as well use it until we got more information. "We should probably make some calls to Japan and see if they know anything about ninjas for hire."

"You really think she's a ninja, Phoenix?"

"I think it's highly possible. Even if she's not a ninja, she's definitely a highly skilled martial artist. That much I know for certain. You don't maintain the kind of control she exhibited when you're thrown fifty or sixty feet over the front of a car you've just rear-ended if you're just a regular Jane. She's probably trained all her life, which also explains how she can keep a cool head while riding a bike at full speed through a busy intersection."

"If it comes down to it, do you think you can take her?"

"I don't know, Kelly. She doesn't have the same value system I have. And that gives her a huge advantage. For example, if it were necessary, she would have shot innocent civilians in the lobby of the hotel with the Uzi she was carrying."

"Too bad it melted in the explosion. We might have gotten a print."

"That's another thing she has going for her—she's lucky."

"She'll make a mistake. They always do."

"Yeah, but we have to catch her before the last hit. Otherwise, she's gone forever."

Simon and Keyth were coming back to the table. They hadn't been gone very long. The fight must have been over quickly, I thought.

"Look who's coming back, Kelly. What do you bet they're gonna want to go upstairs and do it again?"

"No bet. I know Simon, and I know me. Even if it isn't on his mind, it's on mine."

"Mine, too."

Keyth had the strangest look on his face when he reached the table. He sat down and took my hand into his. I looked into his eyes and saw that they were welling with tears. Whatever it was, it was serious.

"It's your father, Phoenix. The Assassin got him."

CHAPTER 33

W ASHINGTON, D.C., was a sweltering 98 degrees when we returned. Keyth's mother, Dorothy, and Savannah met us at Dulles International. Savannah ran to us, screaming, "Mommy and Daddy!" Keyth picked her up and hugged her. I just didn't have the energy. I still felt as if I'd been hit in the stomach with a sledgehammer.

"How was your trip to St. Thomas?" Savannah asked. "I told all the kids in my class where you were."

"We had a good time, honey," I heard Keyth tell her.

Dorothy drove, and my husband and daughter rode up front. I needed the entire back seat to myself. My father was dead, and I had never, ever thought of him dying. And to die at the hands of that homicidal nymphomaniac? Images of law enforcement officers standing over his dead body, making the wisecracks we tended to make, irritated me. I was so hurt that my pain consumed my anger at the killer. Tears rolled down my cheeks like a waterfall. I opened my eyes and saw that my daughter was staring at me. She seemed puzzled by the tears.

She stretched out her arms, indicating that she wanted me to reach for her and pull her into the back seat. I did. I held on to her, and she comforted me. I rocked my daughter, and the anguish I felt gushed forth like a sudden thunderstorm. I cried hard. Soon, Savannah was crying with me. Not long after that, Dorothy and Keyth began to cry, too. The remarkable thing was that my daughter didn't ask me why I was crying.

Amazingly, she just sympathized without explanation. I loved her more, if that were possible, for allowing me to cry without my having to tell her anything.

We were finally home. Keyth brought our bags into the house, then left to take his mother home. When he returned, we all stretched out on our big bed and mourned my father's passing. For the first time since the assassinations began, I didn't think about them or about "Susan Lucci," as we had dubbed her.

CHAPTER 34

I BURIED MY FATHER three days later. In the days before that, as we prepared for the funeral, I tried to remember all that was good about him and us. The time we had spent in China was foremost on my mind. It was there I learned to speak Mandarin and Cantonese. Learning about the Chinese culture was a great experience.

When we returned to the United States, my exposure to Eastern philosophy enabled me to be a better American. From the monks, I had learned the meaning of tolerance. When one is able to look at one's self and see one's self, only then can one know what true tolerance is. It was the ability to see my own attitude, my own selfishness, my own intolerance that allowed me to accept Phoenix first and then those whom I met on the way to self-actualization.

My father was given full military honors because of his time in the Navy. I was surprised to see President Davidson at Arlington Cemetery. Many other representatives from the intelligence community attended, too. While I appreciated the gesture, I wished the President had not come. Everywhere he goes and everything he does becomes a national event.

Consequently, the media was there, filming my family's grief. I wanted to knock their cameras out of my face.

A crowd of people I had never met surrounded the grave site. My father evidently had a lot of friends whom I didn't know. One particular couple really stood out. They weren't talking to anyone, not even to each other.

The man was black, and the woman with him was Asian. They were well dressed and accompanied by two tough-looking black men. I assumed they were bodyguards. I felt my FBI instincts start to kick in, but I didn't want them to. This wasn't the time or the place to think about investigating people. However, it did give me an idea that I would later explore.

The honor guard fired their rifles in unison with military precision. I was startled when I heard the first shot. I looked at Savannah, taking in all the pageantry of her grandfather's funeral. I don't think she fully understood the finality of death yet. At some point, she would wonder; then she would ask her father or me why Granddaddy didn't come to pick her up and take her to the zoo anymore. Keyth and I would deal with her awakening together as a family.

President Davidson personally presented the flag to me, and a million lights flashed in my eyes. Somehow, I knew the pictures would end up in The Washington Post the next day.

"I'm sorry about this media fiasco, Phoenix," Davidson whispered in my ear. I thanked him, and he left me to grieve, taking the members of the media with him.

As he left, I felt for him. He was trying to do a good thing, taking time out to express his condolences. Tomorrow, the media would say his coming here was only a photo opportunity to boost his ratings. The appointment of another conservative black woman to the bench was still haunting him. I admired him for being a strong leader. The last thing the country needed was another president who put his finger in the air to see which way the wind was blowing.

CHAPTER 35

COCO NIMBURU walked into the dojo covered from head to toe in her black ninja uniform—prepared for battle. She knew Phoenix was still grieving over the death of her father, but Coco wanted her back in the game. All of the Washington targets were dead, so she had some time on her hands. Normally, she would've gone out to San Francisco and taken care of the Warren family. But that would be too easy. In Phoenix, she had found an adversary worthy of her talent. After reading her dossier and talking to her father, she had come to respect Phoenix in some small way. In Coco Nimburu's mind, she had caused the grief, and it was up to her to get Phoenix up and on her feet again.

The student-teachers were filming their sparring session, which gave Coco an idea. She stood by quietly, watching to see who was the best. Actually, it really didn't matter who was the best. She had been there five minutes, and not one of them was enough in tune with his or her spiritual side to know she lurked in the shadows, watching, waiting.

After a few more minutes, Coco realized that Karen Monroe was the best of the four; therefore, she would be the last to die. Leaning against the opening onto the practicing floor, she clapped her hands to get their attention.

"May I help you," Karen said, taking the initiative.

"From what I've seen so far, no," Coco told her. "But I can help you."

"We already have a teacher. Grandmaster Perry," Earl Johns said, offended by her arrogance.

"How can you help us?" Karen asked. "There is nothing you can teach us that Grandmaster Perry can't."

"I mentioned nothing about teaching. I said I could help you."

"Help us how?" Karen asked, confused as to where this was going.

"I can help you see God today, rather than tomorrow or the next day." Coco smiled and walked into the midst of them. "Now, who wants to see God first?"

Earl Johns had a club in his hand and drew back to swing. With no wasted movement, Coco hit him in the nose with a straight punch that sent him reeling backward. Blood ran from his nostrils.

"Who's next?" she asked, deadly serious.

They surrounded her, ready to attack. Coco stood there completely relaxed, waiting for any movement. Karen feinted, to see what she would do. Coco angled her body in a defensive posture. Earl Johns, angry because she had embarrassed him, was about to swing the club again. With very little effort, she kicked him in the head, then caught Greg Fisher, who was trying to sneak up behind her with a reverse hook kick to the head. They couldn't even get close to her, and she was just playing with them.

Karen knew they were in trouble. Her instincts told her to run while she could. But her pride would not allow that. She was the best of them, and she would lead them into battle.

Karen kicked at the stranger's head. Coco deflected it with ease, and then she kicked Karen in the head with the same type of kick Karen had just tried—or, as if to show her how it was done. Karen fell to the mat. She had never even seen the kick coming. Then she remembered the words of Grandmaster Perry. "Good Kung Fu isn't seen. It is felt." She stood up quickly and regained her composure. Karen relaxed and allowed her spiritual side to dominate her being. Phoenix had told her that she wasn't far from freedom.

In the meantime, Earl Johns had lost his composure, the worst thing a martial artist can do. He ran at Coco, grabbing her from behind. She snapped her head back into his nose, dazing him.

When he released her, she grabbed his arm and spun around him, then locked his arm. She grabbed a hunk of his hair and snapped his neck. Earl slumped to the floor. Valerie Ryan was next. She came at Coco, fighting sticks in hand. Coco let her swing and then stepped in with a palm strike to the nose. The blow was so powerful that it shoved the bone into her brain, killing her instantly. Greg Fisher came at Coco with a combination of blows and kicks that backed her up. Coco knew that he would do it again because he had had some success. She waited until he was about to start again, then hit him with a spinning kick to the head that dazed him. While he was still woozy, she walked up to him and waited for him to swing. When he did, she ducked and took his legs from under him, then hit him in the balls.

She stood over him, placing a foot on each side of his head, and twisted sharply to the right, breaking his neck.

Karen was ready. Her mind was empty. Coco faced Karen, expecting her to attack. She didn't. Coco could sense that Karen was prepared, but inadequately. The two combatants bowed, keeping their eyes on each other while doing so. Without thought, Karen, completely relaxed, kicked at Coco's head. Though Coco was able to get out of the way, her eyes enlarged with surprise at the speed of the kick. Coco knew that Karen was totally free, probably for the first time as a martial artist. Karen stayed aggressive, kicking in combination, but missing nevertheless.

Karen feinted before attacking again. Because of the speed and power she'd displayed, Coco had to respect the feint, allowing Karen to get close. Surprised by the move, Coco went on the offensive, but it was too late. Karen was already inside. And then it came—the opening. POW—a powerful palm strike to the sternum sent Coco sailing across the room, over the bodies of those she had killed. Karen stepped over the bodies of her fallen friends. Completely focused, she waited for Coco to gather herself from the blow.

Then she attacked more aggressively, striking Coco several times in the face. But her aggression put her in harm's way, and she caught several blows, too. Coco knew it was only a matter of time before the right opening would occur, and she would end it. Coco feinted at Karen's head, waited for her response, and then hit her several times from an angle. Dazed, Karen became sloppy, and Coco hit her with another series of powerful blows. Then she pulled Karen in by her uniform and snapped her neck. After she had killed all of them, Coco went over to the camera and said something into the microphone. Then she took the tape and left the dojo.

CHAPTER 36

D IRECTOR ST. CLAIR, White House Chief of Staff Armando Glover, and President Davidson were discussing the Assassin in the Oval Office. St. Clair had no answers for the president. All he could tell him was that it was a woman who had the nation's capital gripped in fear, wondering who was next.

Hundreds of social events had been canceled, which made the fabled FBI look like a bunch of buffoons. The media played it up big, too. They were doing nightly recaps of the David Koresh fiasco, the Timothy McVeigh mess, the Richard Jewel disaster, and the Oklahoma City and 1993 World Trade Center bombings. They even did a recap on the Hoover years, citing all the excesses of his administration.

Night after night, they meticulously revealed how Hoover shied away from the mob for fear of bureau corruption. They talked about the FBI's failure to protect civil rights activists during the Kennedy administration. The dirt Hoover had on every president from Roosevelt to Nixon was being reviewed and had become fodder for water cooler conversation. And all of this was being laid at the feet of President Davidson because he had nominated another conservative to the Supreme Court. Putting a black woman on the bench meant nothing because of her conservative politics. Even black organizations stood by and watched the carnage.

"What are you doing about the Assassin?" Davidson asked.

"Mr. President, there's only so much we can do," Director St. Clair said, pleading his case. "We don't even know what she looks like, sir. Do you think it's easy for foreign powers to catch our assassins? This woman is good. She leaves no trace."

"How was Special Agent Perry able to find out where she was in one day?"

"She got lucky, sir."

"Maybe she'll get lucky again, St. Clair. Get her back on the case. NOW!"

"Sir, you were at her father's funeral. Do you really think she's in any condition to hunt this woman down?"

"Get her on her feet! I don't care how you do it! I will not leave office with this hanging over my head! The people remember the last thing you did in office. And my legacy is in jeopardy. You see what they did to Jimmy Carter with the hostage situation. This man was able to get Menachem Begin and Anwar Sadat to talk to each other, but what do they remember? The hostage crisis! George Bush was able to win the Gulf War in less than forty days, kept Israel from retaliating against repeated bombing, and what do they remember? 'Read my lips!' That's what they remember. You get Perry back on the job, St. Clair."

"Sir, this is hardly the time to be concerned about your legacy," St. Clair said. "She's killed a senator, the director of the NSA, and a Supreme Court nominee. Besides, you were the one who wanted Perry off the case in the first place."

"Director St. Clair, I'm going to pretend that I didn't hear that," Davidson said, then looked at Chief of Staff Glover. "What's next, Armando?"

St. Clair knew he had been dismissed and walked out in a huff.

CHAPTER 37

PACIFIC HEIGHTS was deathly quiet at two in the morning. Flynn and Ford were in a house across the street from the Warren house, where ten FBI agents were protecting Mr. and Mrs. Warren. The agents had no idea why the Warrens were on the Assassin's hit list. All Flynn and Ford knew was their name and address in San Francisco. Several walked the parameter, and two snipers were in the backyard, hiding in trees. Each unit checked in every fifteen minutes. It would have been better if the Warrens had cooperated and moved to a safe house where Flynn and Ford felt more comfortable protecting them.

Fortunately, Victoria Warren, their thirty-year-old daughter, was out of the country with some girlfriends. At least she was safe, Flynn thought. He took a swallow of his coffee, still keeping a vigilant eye on the Warren house.

Coco Nimburu was in a car just down the street, listening to the agents on the FBI scanner Michelson had provided for her. She could see four agents in teams of two outside. Each time the unit stationed in front of the Warren house checked in, they looked directly across the street. That's where the command post is, Coco deduced. She decided to wait until after the 2:15 check-in. That would give her plenty of time to take care of the guys in the command post, cut off communications, and take out the agents one at a time. It was going to be so easy. They weren't ready for a ruthless assassin who killed without hesitation.

"I think Perry is exaggerating about this so-called female ninja," Flynn told Ford.

"Me, too," Ford said. "No way she could be that good."

"We're ready for her, though," Flynn said. "The Warren house is wired for sound, and we've got four agents inside the house and six outside. She's not foolish enough to try anything with that kind of security."

Coco could hear everything they were saying through the cracked door. She was right outside the command post with her back against the wall—her sniper rifle at her feet. With an eight-edged throwing knife, called a shuriken, in each hand, she waited for the agents across the street to check in. What she heard was typical of law enforcement agents, she thought.

From the time she had begun her training, she had been taught that being outnumbered was an asset, not a liability. Her Chunin (trainers) had taught her that her enemies would be easier to destroy when they outnumbered her. It gave them a false sense of security and ultimately lulled them to sleep—even when they were wide awake. A gun in the hand of an enemy provided the same sense of security and would give her the priceless seconds she needed to kill or escape.

"Time for the boys to check in," Ford said.

A few more seconds passed; then all five units checked in. Coco pushed the door open without making a sound. Flynn, reaching for his coffee cup, saw her reflection in the window. "SHIT!" he shouted without thinking, then went for his gun.

"What the fuck," was all Ford had time to say. Coco threw both her weapons simultaneously. Each shuriken whistled slightly through the air before severing a nerve in the right shoulder of each agent, making it impossible for them to use their trigger fingers. Normally, she would have aimed at their foreheads, but they had disrespected her talent as a skilled assassin. She wanted their heads for that.

In one swift motion, she pulled a scalpel-sharp sword from its sheath and took Flynn's head. Then she spun in a half circle and took Ford's head, too. In the same motion, the sword was back in its sheath before their heads hit the floor.

CHAPTER 38

L OOKING AT the digital timer Flynn and Ford had used to determine when the units were supposed to check in, Coco knew she had thirteen minutes to finish off the six agents outside. Relaxed and focused, she grabbed her silenced rifle and went to the window. The window was old, and it stuck when she tried to raise it. She looked at the timer; she was losing precious seconds wrestling with the window. She was just about to give up when it responded to her pushing.

As it went up, the window made enough noise for the agents across the street to hear. Jokingly, one of the agents said, "What's the matter, Flynn? You spill coffee on the radio or somethin'?"

Coco heard them over the radio, laughing at the questions. She aimed at the one who had asked them. He was still laughing. She squeezed the trigger, and a bullet went into his mouth and out the back of his head. Stunned by what they had just seen, the other three agents looked up at the window, giving Coco clean kill shots. One by one, she shot them all in the head. Then she pulled her throwing knives from the bodies of Flynn and Ford, turned off the communications system, and left the room.

She ran across the street, went to the side of the Warren house, and leaned against the wall. She saw the agents sitting comfortably in trees with rifles equipped with night vision scopes. They were smoking cigarettes and trying to keep warm in the cool night air. Coco threw the first shuriken; it whistled through the air until it collided with flesh.

The sound alerted the other agent. She remained calm and searched for
Coco with her scope. She saw her peering around the corner of the house
and took a shot. The bullet hit the house, sending splintered wood in every
direction.

One of the agents from inside the house called out to ask what was
going on. The agent in the tree was about to warn them when Coco
somersaulted across the yard, making it hard to get a clean shot at her.
Suddenly, a throwing knife entered the forehead of the agent in the tree.
An agent inside the house pulled back the curtain on the door to see what
had happened. Before she got a chance to look, Coco had run up the stairs
and kicked the door off its hinges. She took the dazed agent's weapon and
fired a shot into her head. A woman screamed upstairs while the agents
downstairs fired indiscriminately.

"You see anything?" one said to another.

"No. You?"

Coco tossed a smoke bomb into the living room. When it ignited, thick
clouds filled the room. The smoke alarm rang loudly. Coughing uncontrollably, the agents gave away their positions. Sword in hand, Coco went
into the living room, guided by the sound of their constant coughing. One
agent stood up unexpectedly, firing an Uzi. Glass shattered and fell to the
floor. The agent upstairs was calling for help. Coco was running out of
time. When the agent with the Uzi stopped shooting to change clips, she
threw her sword into his chest and ran forward. The other agent was about
to shoot her when, with one motion, Coco snatched the blade out of the
agent's chest and took the shooter's head before he was able to get off a
shot. Then she did a half spin and took the head of the agent who had had
the blade in his chest.

Coco picked up the Uzi and a couple of clips. As she ran up the stairs, she
discharged the weapon. When she reached the top, she changed clips and
kicked open a bedroom door. No one was there, so she went to the next
door and kicked it open.

The Warrens could hear her approaching their bedroom. The agent
protecting them was in a crouched shooting position, waiting for her to

burst through the door. But it was quiet, no sound or movement at all. He fired several rounds into the door. The bullets hit the wall, finding no flesh. The agent opened the door, looked to the left, then to the right. Seeing nothing, he moved out of the room and stepped on one of several sharp three-inch spikes, strategically placed in front of the door.

He screamed in pain, grabbing the injured foot and hopping on the other. Suddenly a shuriken entered his forehead. With all the opposition vanquished, Coco walked into the bedroom, Uzi in hand. She looked at the elderly black couple. They held each other, staring at her with terror on their faces. Coco hesitated, her eyes softening. Then she heard the distant sirens and regained her strength. She squeezed the trigger, spraying the Warrens with a hail of bullets. Their bodies jerked violently in response. Her work done, Coco left the Warren house and blended into the night.

CHAPTER 39

THE WALK home from Matthew Henson Academy was good for me. Smelling the fresh air, taking in the natural beauty of the area, reminded me that life goes on, no matter who dies or why. But I was tormented by the assassination of my father. What could he possibly have done to warrant a high-priced hit woman's brand of murder? I wondered. Being on suspension had its rewards—I was able to spend more time with my family—but I needed to get back to work on the Assassin case. And if not that case, the Rapist was still out there.

There was no coverage on the news about the rape of Secret Service Agent Joe Rider. If Kelly hadn't told me, I still wouldn't have known about it. The Secret Service covered it up on the theory that if the security chief responsible for protecting the White House could be raped in his own home, some group would decide that they could penetrate the White House and would possibly give it a try. Personally, I think the service was more concerned about its image. The possibility of someone penetrating the White House was something they planned for daily. They didn't want people to know that one of the nation's best soldiers had been raped. As far as I was concerned it was that simple.

The mailman and I spoke as we passed each other. I thought I had better check the mail to see if there was anything in there other than junk mail. I opened the box and pulled out a handful of mail and a videotape. Wondering what could be on the tape, I hurried to the house and put it into the VCR.

Stunned with horror at what I was seeing, I practically fell on the couch. The Assassin was killing my students with ease. She had killed my father and now my students. I didn't believe that any of them would be involved with anything that would put them on her hit list. The only thing that made sense was that she was doing this because she wanted to hurt me.

Maybe my father hadn't done anything either, I thought. She didn't kill him until after we chased her through Washington. Maybe he's dead because of me. Why else would she kill my father and my students? That meant my husband and my daughter could be next. I ran to the telephone and called the school. I told the principal that I was sending some agents to pick up Savannah. While I was still talking to the principal, call waiting interrupted. I clicked over.

"Phoenix, this is Director St. Clair. I know this is a bad time, but we need you back on the Assassin case."

"Yes, sir, but I'm going to need several agents watching my family," I said frantically. "The Assassin put a videotape in my mailbox. She killed four of my best students, sir! Get some people on my family—now!"

I called Kelly and told her we were back in business. We were going to meet at FBI headquarters.

CHAPTER 40

T HE ASSASSIN had left me a message on the tape. Looking directly into the camera, she had announced that she was going to San Francisco. All we could see of her was her penetrating eyes, which were the only thing the ninja uniform didn't cover up. I had the video tech print out a picture of those eyes. My thinking was that maybe we could capture her by studying them, training ourselves to recognize them even if she used colored contact lenses. Using the computer, we were able to change the color of her eyes and print out pictures of them.

Director St. Clair dispatched four field agents to protect Savannah and Keyth, but it seemed inadequate, considering whom they were up against. The Assassin was a martial arts expert and a master of disguise. I would never feel comfortable with her still on the loose. She was prepared to do whatever she had to in any situation.

From what I had seen when Kelly and I had chased her, she was fearless and completely controlled. As far as I was concerned, we needed an army to track and corner her. And even then, we would have to shoot to kill. She wasn't going to be taken easily. That much, I knew for sure. But of course, I could never say that aloud.

Michelson came in and asked me what Kelly and I were doing there. We were suspended, he reminded us. I told him that Director St. Clair had reinstated us that morning. He mumbled something that I couldn't understand.

"Kelly," I began, "I think we oughta look at the rest of those tapes from the Hyatt Regency. If I'm right, she had another room."

"What good would that do?" Michelson asked. "Director St. Clair says she's not even in town. She's in San Francisco."

"Why should we trust what she tells us, Lawrence?" I said, pressing my luck. "Besides, I wanna know who this Winston Keyes guy is. He could have gone to her room. And if he did, that would tell us a whole lot more than what we know right now."

Director St. Clair came into the room and said, "Phoenix, Kelly, take my jet and get to San Francisco. The Assassin took out the whole squad and the Warrens."

"But you had ten agents, plus Flynn and Ford, sir," I said.

"I know, Phoenix," St. Clair said. "I'm going to move your family to a safe house until this is over. Michelson, you see to it."

"Yes, sir," Michelson said, relieved that Phoenix and Kelly weren't going to look at those videotapes that would show him going into the Assassin's room. "I'm on top of it," he told the Director.

CHAPTER 41

S AN FRANCISCO'S weather was freezing compared to Washington's, but I wasn't going to complain. Inspector Franklin picked us up at the airport, and we checked into South San Francisco's Embassy Suites Hotel. Soon we were on our way to the crime scene in Pacific Heights. I hadn't been to the city in so long that I'd almost forgotten how much fun I'd had there when my dad and I had returned to America. We had stayed there two weeks, enjoying the sights.

Inspector Franklin was the liaison officer with the San Francisco Police Department assigned to assist our unit at the Warren house. I got the feeling that Franklin would be going to church this week to thank God that she wasn't on duty the night the Assassin paid our guys a visit. She warned us about the gruesome crime scene. "A couple of years ago, Antowain Smith, a high-ranking member of the Chiefs street gang, was decapitated the same way," she told us. "His head still hasn't been found. Had she taken the heads of her victims, I would have thought that the Assassin was the one who had committed that crime, too."

Pacific Heights was just as I remembered it. I think I appreciated the beauty of the city more at thirty-six than I had at eighteen. Had eighteen years really passed? I asked myself. It didn't seem like it. It seemed like my dad and I had just come back a couple of years ago.

I made myself a promise to bring Savannah there when this was all over. I wanted to show her all the places my dad and I had visited before she was born. When I thought about my dad just then, the reminder of his murder overwhelmed me. But joy filled my heart when my memories guided me back to the time he and I went to Pier 39. He bought me cotton candy and hot dogs. It had been such a precious time for me.

But I wasn't in the City by the Bay for a visit. I was here to get a lead on the Assassin. We entered the townhouse across the street from the Warren home where the command post had been set up and saw the bodies of Flynn and Ford on the carpeted floor. Their blood looked as if it had been pumped out of their decapitated bodies. Both Flynn and Ford also had wounds in their right shoulders. I stooped down to get a better look. I knew what kind of weapon she had used.

"Kelly," I said. "What do you think?"

"Shuriken?"

"Yep. She's carrying all the tricks of the trade."

"I get the feeling she's just playing with us, Phoenix."

"Me, too. She could be anywhere. We have to stop following her around and get ahead of her somehow. I'm thinking we need to find out who Winston Keyes is."

"How do you propose we do that?"

"We gotta find Victoria Warren. Maybe she knows who's behind this. If she does, she may be motivated to help us."

"According to her parents, she won't return from Europe for another couple of weeks," Franklin said. "The Warrens refused to tell us the name of the hotel where she is staying. They didn't want her coming home because the FBI thought someone was trying to kill them. They thought she would be safer in Europe."

"Well, you can bet the Assassin is going after the next target. Some guy named Sterling Wise. I think he's a lawyer here."

"I know who you're talking about," Franklin said. "He won't be hard to find. You guys remember the Nehemiah Samuelson case a couple years back?"

"Yeah," Kelly said. "Killed his partner and got off, right?"

"That's him. Sterling Wise was his lawyer. He's a big-time sports agent now."

"You know where we can find him?" I asked.

"Sure. I can take you to his office."

CHAPTER 42

WISE CHOICE SPORTS was the name of the agency Sterling Wise headed. Soon after he had won the Samuelson case, gaining national recognition, he had become a sports agent, leaving the unsavory entanglements of being a defense attorney behind.

Inspector Franklin dropped us in front of the building and went to get coffee, promising to meet us at Sterling Wise's office. Kelly and I entered the building where his office was located and walked to the elevator. I pushed the up button. While we waited for the elevator doors to open, I was thinking about all the deaths. What possible reason would there be to kill so many people, so quickly, and not be concerned about all the publicity?

The doors opened, and we stepped into the elevator. I pushed the button that would take us to the top floor. Just before the doors closed, a gentleman stuck his brass-handled cane in. Immediately, the doors retracted.

"Ladies," the man said. "I hope you don't mind riding with a chap from Great Britain." He was a little shorter than me, with expertly cut gray hair and a gray goatee. He was wearing a black three-piece suit, with a matching derby, a white turtleneck, and a monocle. He had to be about eighty.

"Not at all," Kelly said, friendly as usual.

"I see we're going to the same floor," he continued. "This cannot be a coincidence. Two beautiful women and me taking a similar journey together. It's the stuff dreams are made of."

I ignored the old fool and continued my thoughts about the Assassin.

Then I noticed that he was about to pinch Kelly's ass. I couldn't believe it. So I watched him; sure enough, he pinched.

Kelly turned around. With a smile on her face, she said, "Stop that before you give yourself a heart attack."

"It's one of the things a man my age can get away with." He chuckled. "I remember back during World War II, I got shot to hell and sent back to England. The nurse who looked after me had the most delectable ass. She was a dog, but her ass was splendid. And from time to time, she allowed me a few excesses, too. I love being old. Women let you get away with murder."

I shook my head. If he had done that to me, I would have slapped that derby off his head. I didn't give a damn how old he was. But that's where Kelly and I were different. I was the straight man in our duo. I liked the fact that she could take something like that in stride, though.

The doors opened, and the old man allowed us to leave first. Maybe there's a gentleman in there somewhere after all, I thought.

We entered the outer office of the Wise Choice Sports Agency and were greeted by a young black woman seated behind a circular desk. The English gentleman had come into the office, also. He stood behind us, graciously waiting for us to conclude our business.

"Hello, I'm Special Agent Phoenix Perry, and this is Agent McPherson." We showed her our credentials. "I'm looking for Sterling Wise."

"I'm sorry, Agent Perry, but Sterling and Tiffany are out of the office for about a week or so. Football season starts in September. They're in Denver right now, but they're going to be traveling all over the country."

"Well, does he have an itinerary?" I asked. "It's a matter of life and death."

"I'm sure he does, but he never tells me. He doesn't like his clients to know where he is. They're all prima donnas. You wouldn't believe how they act during contract talks. They all think they're the most important clients he has. So they pester him day and night. He does call in, though. When he does, I'll tell him you need to speak with him right away."

"Does he have a cell phone?"

"Yes, but I can't give you the number."

"Well, do you have an address in Denver where he can be reached?"

"No, and if I had it, I couldn't give it to you," she said firmly. "Give me your number, and he'll call you when he can."

"Ma'am, do you understand that this is a matter of life and death?" I asked.

She stared at me for a few seconds before saying, "I may be just a receptionist, but the job requires that I not be hearing impaired. Now, as I said, I will give him the message, and he'll call you when he can. But don't hold your breath; he's busy. Being an agent is a twenty-four-hour-a-day job. That's something you should understand, Special Agent Perry. Crime isn't committed from nine to five, is it?"

She had a point, but she had also gotten on my nerves. The attitude wasn't necessary. I looked at Kelly. She shook her head, knowing I was planning to roast-beef her. I agreed with her. We would need her later. Kelly took over. It was good cop/bad cop time.

"We can be reached at this number," Kelly said, giving the receptionist a card.

While Kelly was talking, it occurred to me that the English gentleman had been perfectly quiet. I turned around but he was gone.

"Excuse me, but when did the gentleman behind us leave?" I interrupted.

"A couple of minutes ago."

"Kelly! The old man was the Assassin! Let's go!"

CHAPTER 43

WE BOLTED through the door and ran into an open elevator. The Assassin was making us look like idiots. She didn't respect us at all, waltzing into the same elevator, talking to us, feeling Kelly's ass. This was humiliating. I looked at Kelly and shook my head.

"What, Phoenix?"

"And you let her feel you up."

Kelly laughed. "The bitch is bold. You gotta give her that much."

"You know we gotta keep this to ourselves, right? If Michelson hears about this, he's going to have a meltdown."

The elevator doors opened, and we sprinted to the glass doors, guns in the air, almost running into people. Once we hit the street, we looked in both directions, but the Assassin was gone. I was mad as hell. But I wasn't sure if I was angry because she had nerve or because I hadn't recognized her.

What good did it do to print out pictures of our suspect's eyes if I wasn't going to look into the eyes of the people I came in contact with? I thought about my husband and Savannah. If she could do what she did last night to twelve agents and walk right up to the special agent in charge, what chance did we have of catching her?

"Let's go back up to the office, Kelly. No more Mrs. Nice Guy."

"Roast-Beef?" Kelly asked.

"Roast-Beef."

We burst into the office, our faces contorted. "Now look, you fucking idiot," I shouted, "the woman who just left here is going to kill your boss if we don't stop her! Do you understand? Now get him on the phone—right now! Or I'm hauling your ass in for obstructing a federal investigation."

She picked up the telephone and dialed his number. Then she looked at me and said, "It's ringing." She was scared, and I was glad. If that's what it took to save the poor bastard's life, so be it. "His voice mail is on."

As scared as she was, I thought it best to let her leave the message. Maybe if he heard the fear in her voice, he would give us a call. Her voice quivered when she spoke. I thought, that's perfect. If that doesn't prompt him to call us, nothing will.

CHAPTER 44

THE EMBASSY SUITES HOTEL was an oasis as far as I was concerned. It had all the comforts of home, and I needed that right now. After being humiliated and toyed with by the Assassin, I longed for a hot bath and the quiet of my room.

I had nearly made a fool out of myself with the hotel desk clerk. I kept staring at her eyes, making sure she wasn't the Assassin. She thought I was a lesbian, the way I kept staring, and told me what time she was getting off that night. That's when I knew I was losing control. I had become obsessed with catching the Assassin. Who could blame me?

She was slippery and frustrating, but she was going to make a mistake, I told myself. She had already made one by leaving the laptop out at the Capitol Hill Hyatt Regency, and she'd make another. Playing with us today was a mistake, too. We didn't catch her, but the odds were with us.

Susan Lucci—we still called her that—in addition to being the most ruthless killing machine I've ever encountered, was a thrill seeker. Her penchant for sexual bondage was another sign of her seeking thrills that only satisfied her momentarily. I wondered if she was nearing burnout.

I felt the water in the tub. It was hot, just the way I like it. I picked up the telephone and called the safe house. Michelson had moved Keyth and Savannah to a house in Bethesda. I knew they were safe, but only because I knew the Assassin was in San Francisco. If I hadn't had the comfort of knowing she was three-thousand miles away from my family, I don't know if I would have been able to sleep, even after a hot bath.

I knew I would sleep like a baby that night. My family was safe. Kelly and I had survived another day on the job. That's what it's really about. Doing the job and going home in one piece to your family at night.

Agent James answered the phone. He was a by-the-book, twenty-year veteran. Some people didn't like that about him, but my family's life was in his hands, and I was glad he was assigned the detail. I trusted him. He would die before letting anything happen to my family.

"James, this is Phoenix Perry. I would like to speak with my husband, please."

"Yes, ma'am. Authorization code, please."

James knew my voice, but that's what I mean. He didn't take any chances. It reassured me that my husband and daughter were safe.

"Alpha and Omega. The beginning and the end," I said. It was my way of acknowledging the Almighty for helping me through another day on the job.

"Just a second," I heard him say. A few seconds later, Keyth answered. "Hello," his deep voice bellowed. I stepped into the hot water and eased in gingerly.

"Hi, sweetheart," I said. "How's Savannah?"

"She was a little overwhelmed with all of the security at first, but she's growing on everyone. Just like you do."

"Ahhhh, that's sweet of you to say."

"I miss you, baby. When do you think you'll be home?"

"I'm not sure. But you guys can relax. She's out here, just like she said she would be." I laughed. "Maybe we've got an honest murderer on our hands, if you can believe that."

"It is funny, isn't it? Listen, it's a madhouse now that your dad isn't around. It's going to be tough to keep the business going without him. He had all the contacts. The clients don't know me. I really think the business is going to need you and your name to stay afloat. I don't mean to put pressure on you, baby, but please consider coming into the business after this case, okay?"

"Okay, Keyth. I've been thinking about it for some time now. Daddy told me that he wanted me to come in with him and make it a family business. He wanted it to be something we could leave to our children after us."

"Does that mean we're going to have some more babies?"

I was quiet for a moment or two. My husband had wanted more children for years, but I just didn't see how I could do it. A working mother, especially an FBI agent, has so much pressure on her. I didn't like leaving Savannah as much as I did, but the demands of the job required it. And I'm not a desk jockey. I like to be out there on the street, hunting down brutal, unrelenting murderers like our friend Susan Lucci.

"I don't know, Keyth. Probably."

"You mean it!" he shouted, exploding with joy.

I loved making him happy. He was my soul mate, my most intimate friend. I trusted him implicitly. We were happy and content with each other. That doesn't mean that Keyth never got on my nerves. Of course he did, leaving socks and shoes everywhere, not putting the cap back on the toothpaste, and leaving the television on when he knew he was falling asleep on the couch.

But all of that paled in comparison to how he makes me feel. He's dependable, loyal, ambitious, and intelligent, and, more importantly, he knows how to ring my bell in the bedroom consistently and often. A lot of women try to downplay the sex, but these are the same women who are always complaining about their husbands.

"Yeah, I mean it," I said. "I'm not saying this is my last case. I'm not making that commitment at this point. What I'm saying is that I'm finally giving it serious consideration. The Assassin has pretty much closed down my school."

"Yeah, I heard about that. I'm so sorry, baby. You got any idea why she did that?"

"No, but it means that whatever is going on, Daddy may not have been involved in anything. He may have been just another casualty in her effort to get at me."

"Don't let it get personal, Phoenix." Whenever he called me by my first name, I knew he was very serious about what he was saying to me.

"Too late, Keyth. It's way too late for that." My anger was bubbling over. "Not only did she kill Daddy and my friends, but she wiped out seven years of time I put into training those students. Karen was almost there. This vicious killer put my job in jeopardy and closed the doors on my business. Thanks to her, my options are dwindling. Yeah, it's personal, Keyth."

"I went to see your dad's lawyer like you asked me to," he said, changing the subject. He knew my moods so well—another thing I loved about him. "Your dad left you quite a bit of money and more than half of the business. You've got some big decisions to make. I won't bore you with all the details right now. I know you've got a lot on your mind. But when this thing with the Assassin is over, we gon' have a talk, hear?"

I like it when he's firm with me. Keyth knows I can kick his ass, but he's never backed down in an argument. He takes no prisoners when he's mad at me.

"Okay, but when it's over," I said, "not before. Is Savannah asleep yet?"

"Yes. It's almost eleven here."

"Yeah, I know. I was just hoping she might be up," I said. "Tell her I love her, okay?"

"Okay," he said quietly.

"Are you mad?" He sounded like it.

"I'm more worried than anything else. I saw the news today. That woman is lethal, lopping off heads and shit like the Grim Reaper."

"Don't worry, Keyth. She could have killed me twice already and didn't. She's a killing machine, no doubt about that, but she kills with a purpose."

"Why did she kill all the agents? What was the purpose of that?"

"I don't know, probably to demonstrate her skill or something. I'll be sure and ask next time I see her, though."

"Okay, smart-ass," he said. "Talk to you later."

"I love you, Keyth."

"I love you, too."

CHAPTER 45

I N A SUITE one floor up from Phoenix Perry's room, using high-powered binoculars, Coco Nimburu had seen Phoenix through the huge picture window each Embassy Suites hotel room provides. Michelson had told her that the dynamic duo would be staying at the South San Francisco Embassy, so she had booked three rooms for the night, using Susan Lucci and two other names. Posing as a maid, she had bugged both agents' rooms and telephones while they were at the crime scene in Pacific Heights. She listened to Phoenix and Keyth's conversation, formulating a plan to kidnap him and Savannah. And now she had Phoenix's authorization code. It was so easy. Coco was having so much fun. She could hear Phoenix in the tub, splashing around like a fish on a hook. The game would continue when she finished bathing.

The man who had taken Coco's bags to her suite promised to return when his shift was over. She needed a little sexual healing. She hadn't ravaged anyone last night at the Warren house—not sexually, anyway. In a little while, her chosen playmate would arrive, and she would give him the ride of his life. Unlike so many before him, he would get to brag about it. But until that time, she was going to have a talk with her nemesis, woman to woman. Phoenix was getting out of the tub. She was singing an old Rose Royce tune, "I Wanna Get Next to You."

Coco could see Phoenix at the huge picture window, about to close the curtains. She was wearing a white terry-cloth robe. When the curtains were closed, Phoenix turned off the light and went into the bedroom. Coco sat on the sofa, opened an electronically locked suitcase and took out a special telephone that gave false locations when a trace on it was activated. She put on a headset and called Phoenix's room.

"Hello."

"Cheers, Phoenix!" Coco said, using the British accent she'd used earlier. "We had fun today, didn't we?"

Phoenix's heart pounded. She sat up, unable to believe the gall of this woman. She wasn't prepared to talk to her. How did she know where I was staying? Phoenix wondered.

"Well, say something," Coco said in Cantonese, snapping Phoenix out of the fog she was in. The Assassin was speaking Cantonese to see if she could really speak the language as her dossier purported. That way, when she kidnapped Keyth and Savannah, she could be sure no one was listening. If Phoenix could speak Cantonese fluently, she could probably speak Mandarin as well. Phoenix was hers to do with as she pleased. When she was ready, when Phoenix had been taught a lesson, they would meet face to face.

Answering in Cantonese, Phoenix said, "So you've been to the Orient." The martial arts were practiced all over the world, which meant having the skill of a ninja didn't necessarily make the Assassin Japanese.

"Many times. So many people to kill, so little time to kill them," Coco joked.

"What's your name?"

"Let's just stick with Susan for a while, shall we, Phoenix?"

"You have me at a disadvantage. You know my name and apparently a lot more than I gave you credit for."

"It is true. I do have the advantage. But, somebody has to have it. Might as well be me." She laughed.

"Can you hold on for a second? I put some popcorn in the microwave."

"Sure, take your time," Coco said and went to the window. She watched Phoenix run next door to McPherson's room. She could hear every word they were saying.

136

"I've got her on the phone," Phoenix was telling McPherson. "Get a trace on the line."

Coco laughed. This was so funny. It was going to be even funnier when they found out where she was. Phoenix ran back to the telephone. "Hello," she said, a little winded.

"You sound like you're out of breath," Coco said, still speaking Cantonese. "I told you to take your time. How's the popcorn?"

"It burned. Had to throw it away."

"That's too bad. Now, where were we?"

"Why are you killing people?"

"You'll find out soon enough. Shall we discuss the death of your father or your students first?" Phoenix kept her composure. Coco had struck a nerve by mentioning the murders of her father and students so casually. "Don't you want to kill me for that?"

Ignoring the question, Phoenix asked, "Why did you kill them?"

Kelly burst into the room and whispered, "She's everywhere. We have her in San Francisco, London, Rome, New York, and fifty other places, all at the same time."

"Your dad's death was contractual. That's all I can tell you now. Your students, well, that was personal."

"Well, why not come after me? Why the students?" Phoenix yelled into the telephone.

"Temper, temper. You must be frustrated about the trace, huh? You've got to know by now that I am not stupid."

"Well, what the hell do you want?"

"Ever go to the movies?

"Yes. And?"

"Ever see *Heat* with Robert De Niro and Al Pacino?"

"Sure, I've seen it."

"Remember the scene when Pacino wanted to have a face-to-face with De Niro?"

"So that's what you want, a face-to-face?"

"Eventually. But right now, let's talk to each other."

"You never answered why you killed my students. You said it was personal. But why would a professional like you let it get personal?"

"Have you let it get personal, Phoenix?" She paused and waited for an answer, but Phoenix remained silent. "In our business, these things happen from time to time. But to answer your question, I killed them to get you back into the game. You were having such a pity party about your father's death. You were falling into the black hole of self-doubt. I want the woman who chased me through the streets of Washington. I want that relentless woman who never gives up."

"Why do I interest you so much?"

"Because you scared me that day, and I liked it. I've never felt so alive. I wasn't sure I was going to get away. I had become lazy—a cop, if you will." She laughed, then continued. "I was arrogant, too comfortable. You have awakened my spirit of adventure. I want you to do something for me."

"Yeah? What's that?"

"All in good time, Phoenix. All in good time."

"I assume you're a movie buff, considering the De Matteo disguise you wore that day. Must have cost a fortune."

"Yes. My disguises are quite expensive. But they are absolutely flawless."

"Who makes them for you?"

"A guy I fuck from time to time. Works for Paramount Studios."

Phoenix shook her head. "You mentioned Pacino and De Niro, and you used Susan Lucci's name."

"What does that tell you about me, Phoenix?"

"It tells me you want to be known, yet you won't tell me your name. A vast contradiction. Are you conflicted? Do you want to be famous, yet stay hidden behind your ninja uniform and your superior ability to become whomever you want?"

"You are so good at this. What would you say if I told you that you looked good enough to eat when I told you which way the blonde had run in Union Station? I had to restrain myself from grabbing the back of your head and tasting your sweet tongue."

"So you're bisexual as well?"

"Isn't every woman? Don't you ever wonder why it's so easy to judge the appearance of another woman, her shape, her manner of dress, etcetera?"

"No. I call it confidence in one's own sexuality."

"Exactly! Now you understand me. I take what I want. I live as I please. If a man pleases me, I will have him. If a woman like you attracts me, I will have her. No contradiction. Confidence only."

"Why did you shoot some agents and chop the heads off of others? Was there some significance to that?"

"Depends on the situation. Flynn and Ford disrespected my art. I listened to them talk about what you had told them. You had warned them about my skill, did you not?"

"Yes."

"Not only didn't they take what you said seriously, they didn't take me seriously. All those agents were sitting ducks, waiting to be killed. But Flynn and Ford really pissed me off. So I took their heads."

"What about my father? Why him?"

"You bore me with your questions, Phoenix. I have given you an opportunity to talk to the most lethal weapon you'll ever encounter and this is what you ask me?"

"How about you tell me what you want me to know. That way you won't be bored. Obviously, you want to talk about yourself. Yet you still refuse to give me your name."

"I guess it really doesn't matter now. This is my last contract. I will tell you everything I can to help you find and kill me. I'll even tell you why. My name is Coco Nimburu of the Nimburu clan, one of only a few families who survived the slaughter of ninja clans more than five centuries ago. I have AIDS.

"The protease inhibitors seemed to work for a while, but several physicians have told me they don't understand why the inhibitors don't work in my system. I can feel myself starting to decay. I refuse to go through the horror of disintegration. I have chosen you as my executioner. You are the only one of two people I respect enough for the job. The other woman was at your father's funeral. You may have seen her. She was Asian, but her husband is black. Do you recall seeing her?"

"Yes. Who is she? What's her name? What do they have to do with this?"

"Plenty, Phoenix. Plenty. As for knowing who they are, well, you don't need to know that at this point. You'll find out soon enough. Anyway, I probably would have gone on killing for a price, but now is a good time to die. And along the way, I will enjoy everything that life has to offer."

"What makes you think I'll kill you?" Phoenix asked, startled that the Assassin was revealing so much.

"I will kill you if you don't. You will die, knowing that you could have stopped me. And I will go on killing until my last breath if the woman I just told about doesn't. Or until I find another adversary worthy of killing me."

"So that's why you killed my father and my students? You killed innocent people to get me to kill you?"

"Nobody's innocent, Phoenix. Not you, not me, not your students, and certainly not your precious father. We are all guilty before God. Your father told me that he knew one day someone would come to kill him. I gave him a great sendoff. I rode him like a thoroughbred. Then I snapped his neck clean. He didn't feel a thing. I was merciful."

Sensing that she had finally learned something about the Assassin, Phoenix seized the opportunity.

"So the victims you killed by snapping their necks, you killed for mercy's sake?"

"Yes."

"Then Judge Taylor, Clayton Pockets, Scott Gordon, my father were all mercy killings?"

"Yes. Otherwise, it would have been brutal like it was for your colleagues who disrespected my art."

Phoenix had the answer now. All she had to do was find out why Jennifer Taylor's murder was merciful and why Martha Blevins' murder wasn't. Both were women. But Martha was beaten to a pulp before being shot to death.

"Hmmmm," Phoenix muttered.

"I see you're getting the picture now. I like you, Phoenix, so I'm going to do you a favor when I go back to Washington. Don't worry. I won't be going back for a while. You know by now you can take my word for that. But when I get back, I'm going to kill the Rapist you can't seem to find.

Every clue you need is right in front of you. Who knows, Keyth may be next on his list."

"You know about that?"

"I know about everything, Phoenix. Well, I must go. I have an appointment with a young man. I'm going to fuck his brains out. No, it isn't Sterling. Not tonight, anyway. Better hope you get to him before I do. Dead men tell no tales."

And with that, she disconnected.

CHAPTER 46

I SMILED when I looked at Kelly, who had sat quietly throughout, no doubt wondering what was being said. Kelly had seen that look on my face many times before and knew that I had figured out something important to the case. Eager to hear what I had learned, she leaned forward and smiled, too.

"What is it? What did she tell you, Phoenix?"

"Kelly, we gotta find out more about Judge Taylor and Senator Blevins. That's going to lead us to who's behind all of this."

"She told you that?"

"Not in so many words. We were on the right track all along. I believe that what we saw on the tapes at the Four Seasons was exactly what it looked like."

"What do you mean?" Kelly looked puzzled.

"Think about it, Kelly. What did we see? It was complicated, yet so simple. Everything we need to solve this thing is staring us right in the face, but we've been so busy following the Assassin around that we didn't have time to do the simple stuff, like watching all the security tapes. Every time we tried, someone else was killed and we'd go to investigate. The murders were unintentional diversions. If there had been only the one murder, we would probably be closer to catching Coco Nimburu."

"So she told you her name?"

"Yeah, and that she's got AIDS. She's got nothing to lose. We won't find her in the computer, but we'll run her name anyway."

"I'm confused. What did we see on the tapes that was so obvious?"

"We saw a chauffeur going into an expensive suite at the Four Seasons. Moments later, a rich-looking woman, hiding her identity, goes to the chauffeur's room. They're in the room for six hours, and then Judge Taylor arrives. The two women argue loudly enough to be heard in the next suite. The video shows them pointing their fingers in each other's faces. A few hours later, Judge Taylor is dead. And Winston Keyes' last call was to the Capitol Hill Hyatt Regency. Now, I ask you, who can afford to pay someone of the Assassin's caliber?"

"The rich woman. But why?"

"That I haven't figured out yet. But we need to review those tapes as soon as we can."

"Why not call headquarters and tell them to watch the tapes. That way we can get a head start."

"No way, Kelly. I think she has someone inside the bureau working for her. She practically told me as much. She knows too much about me, the operations, and where our people are. How did she know we were here? I don't trust anyone except you. We gotta keep this to ourselves. We're going to check outta here now and get to Denver."

"But we don't know where to find Sterling Wise there."

"I know. But we do know why he's there. We'll just go to the franchise and find out from them. We're not waiting for our killer to lead us anymore. We're going to be aggressive from here on out."

CHAPTER 47

T WO HOURS LATER, Kelly and I were in the lobby checking out. I called headquarters and had them run a check on Coco Nimburu. As I had predicted, we didn't have anything on her. I charged the hotel bill to my FBI expense account and was about to leave when I stopped in my tracks. I had had an epiphany.

"She's here, Kelly," I said, and walked back to the desk. "Do you have a Susan Lucci registered here?"

"I'll check," the clerk said. "Yes, she's in room 1196."

"Call the police and ask for Inspector Franklin. Tell her the Assassin is here. I need a key to that room."

"It's going to take a second. I have to program a card for that room."

The desk clerk inserted an electronic card into a slot on the computer, hit a few keys on the keyboard, and handed me the programmed card. We took the elevator up to the eleventh floor with our weapons out. The doors opened, and we hustled over to Room 1196. My heart pounded in my chest, threatening to explode. I looked at Kelly. She nodded.

I put the key in the slot, and we burst into the room. No one was in the living room area, but we could see a naked man tied to the bed. I put my weapon back in its holster. I knew Coco Nimburu was in the wind again. We walked into the bedroom. She had left me a note in Cantonese on the dead man's chest that read:

I was going to let him live, Phoenix, but he forgot the condoms. As you can see by the color of his balls, he went blissfully. I couldn't let him go through life with the virus. See how merciful I can be? HA, HA, HA. Life sure is funny, isn't it? You never know what's going to happen next. Remember what I told you. If you don't kill me, I will kill you. I will encourage you again along the way.

Yours truly,

Coco

CHAPTER 48

CYNTHIA CHARLES always swore when she and Sterling made love. She couldn't help herself. Profanity just found its way out of her mouth. The closer she got to the peak of excitement, the louder and more profane she became.

"Ring my bell. Ring my goddamned bell, Sterling," Cynthia purred. "Bang the goo. Oh, bang the goo. Just like that, baby. Just like that. Make it talk. Make-it-talk! What's it saying to you, Daddy?"

Sterling wanted to say, "It's saying, shut the hell up. I'm trying to bust a nut," but he held his peace.

They were in her bedroom on the king-sized bed. The dark room was scantily lit with jasmine-scented candles. The CD carousel was filled with the jazz artists George Howard, Najee, and David Sanborn playing soft, romantic tunes. Cynthia's perfume filled Sterling's nostrils. Her scent was intoxicating. They were moving fast and out of control. Cynthia screamed loudly, clutching the black satin sheets.

"You can get off me now," Cynthia told him after a few minutes.

"Let me lay in it a minute," Sterling said, gasping for air.

He was in town to get a new contract for Daunte King, Denver's star quarterback. But he still had two years left on a four-year contract, and the publicity associated with his arrest would make it difficult to negotiate a new deal.

King was a lightning rod for trouble; this time the police had hauled him in for beating up his live-in girlfriend. On top of that, he had tested positive for cocaine.

Sterling was on his back now, and Cynthia rolled out of the bed. She took the used condom off him and went into the adjacent bathroom. After flushing the condom down the toilet, she turned on the faucet. A moment later, she came out of the bathroom with a warm black face towel and cleaned their juices off him. As she wiped him clean, he felt himself desiring her again. She looked at him and said, "Don't you ever get enough?"

"Not when I'm in Denver. I think it's the altitude or something."

"Altitude, my ass. It's that damn Viagra!" She laughed. "Give me a chance to bask in the glow. I'll take care of you later. You hungry?"

"Yeah."

"What would you like?"

"I gotta taste for some breakfast. You know, bacon, eggs. That sorta thing."

"It's a little late in the evening for breakfast, don't you think? It's almost 10:15," she said, looking at the clock.

"So? What's wrong with having a late breakfast?"

"Nothin', I guess."

CHAPTER 49

"AGENT PERRY, this is Tiffany Quinn, Sterling Wise's personal assistant. How can I help you?"

Finally, I thought, we had gotten ahead of the Assassin. "I need to speak with him, Ms. Quinn. It's a matter of life and death—his, to be specific."

"He's on another line, right now, Agent Perry. Can you hold?"

"Yes."

★★★

Sterling had kept Cynthia Charles up half the night and she had overslept. She enjoyed their time together but decided it was time to break off their eleven-year fling. He wasn't the settling down type, and even if he was, she had always known that she could never get serious with him. Besides, she had met a guy whom she thought had serious husband potential. Now that she had had her last fling with Sterling, she could move on and concentrate on the man she hoped would be the one she'd been waiting for.

Cynthia didn't dare tell Sterling about the potential husband—just in case it didn't work out. Sterling was good to her. He took her on expensive cruises and vacations two or three times a year. And everything was always first-class. She wasn't about to blow an eleven-year thing with Sterling for a guy she hadn't even bedded yet. For all she knew, the potential may not be able to handle his business in the bedroom.

Finally ready to leave her home, Cynthia opened the front door and found a strange woman standing there. "Whatever it is you're selling, I don't have time right now. I'm late for work."

Coco pulled out her silenced Makarov and put it to Cynthia's forehead. "Sure you do, Cynthia. This will only take a little while. And seeing that that's all you've got left in this world, I'd be a little nicer if I were you."

Pressing the gun harder against Cynthia's forehead, Coco pushed her backward, walked into the house, and closed the door. Cynthia couldn't believe this was happening to her. She had heard all the statistics about someone being robbed every five minutes, but she never dreamed it would happen to her.

"I've got money. That's what you want, isn't it?"

"Why do they always think it's about money?" Coco said. "This is about your lover, Sterling Wise. Where is he?"

"He's not here!"

Coco slapped her on the cheek with the gun. "Did I ask you if he was here? I said, 'Where is he?'"

"I don't know! I don't know!" Cynthia screamed. Her face was throbbing. "He left early."

Coco slapped her several more times with the gun. Cynthia's cheeks were swelling. "Now, one more time, Cynthia. I know you know where he is or where he's going. I can keep this up all day. Can you?"

"Okay, okay, okay," Cynthia repeated. "Just don't hit me again."

Coco put the gun away, hoping it would lull Cynthia into thinking that Coco wouldn't kill her if she told her where Sterling was. "Okay, Cynthia. I put the gun away. Now, tell me where he is."

"Are you going to kill him?"

Coco kicked Cynthia in the head, and she fell to the floor. Cynthia wasn't taking the situation seriously. Coco had asked her several times where Sterling was, had slapped her around with the gun, and she still wasn't cooperating. That's why Coco preferred the men. She could just whip out the needles, promise them pleasure, which she delivered, and they told her everything she wanted to know. But women, they were different, always asking questions, taking unnecessary punishment.

Then Coco dragged Cynthia to the bedroom by her hair, screaming,

"You bitch! I was going to be merciful, but now I'm going to kill you slow! And you're still going to tell me where he is! By the time I get finished with you, you're going to tell me everything! You're going to tell me so much, I'm going to have to torture you to shut you up!"

✳✳✳

"Agent Perry, Sterling Wise here. I'm sorry I didn't return your call sooner, but my cell batteries died and I had to pick some up today. Now, what's this about?"

"Sir, I have reason to believe your life is in danger," Phoenix said. "There's an assassin searching for you. This is no ordinary assassin. She's killed about twenty people in less than two weeks—fourteen in one night."

"What? Why is she coming after me?"

"I was hoping you could tell me. Who would want you dead? Maybe a case you lost? Perhaps a client from the past? The Assassin is being well paid, I suspect. Therefore, it would have to be someone wealthy. I believe it's a woman paying the bill. Can you think of anyone with enough money to pay a high-priced assassin to kill you?"

The moment Phoenix said she thought it was a wealthy woman, Sterling knew who was trying to have him killed. He had handled a delicate matter for her and the Warren family right after the Samuelson case. He feared for the Warrens.

"Agent Perry," Sterling said soberly, "I can't tell you who's trying to kill me. I could be disbarred. Attorney-client privilege is still in effect. But I know why she's doing this. Please, can you tell someone in San Francisco to get to Pacific Heights? She'll be going after the Warren family next."

"Too late, sir."

"Oh, no!" Sterling said. "She killed them all?"

"Everybody except Victoria Warren. She happened to be out of the country at the time."

"Thank God! At least she's safe."

"This woman was able to kill twelve agents, sir. Let me take you to some-place safe."

"Someplace safe? She killed twelve agents and you still think you can protect me?"

"It would help to know who your client is. Maybe we can track her down before the Assassin finds you. She can call it off."

"No chance of that, Agent Perry. You have no idea what this is about, do you? You don't know what the stakes are, do you?"

"Where are you, sir? I can come and pick you up right now. I have Director St. Clair's jet."

"My limo is pulling into the airport now. Where are you?"

"I'm already here. I can meet you at any gate you say, sir. I really need to speak with you."

"Okay, meet us at Gate 47."

CHAPTER 50

WE HUSTLED to Gate 47. This was the big break we had been hoping for. We had beaten Coco Nimburu to her next target. If I could get Sterling Wise to talk, we could find the rich woman and put an end to the carnage. Kelly and I made it to Gate 47 in record time. We looked for Sterling. He had said that he was a tall black man wearing a blue suit and that his assistant Tiffany was a white brunette wearing a wine-colored pantsuit and pumps.

Kelly spotted them. "There they are."

But suddenly I felt the presence of the Assassin. She was here. But how? I wondered. How could she know so much? Someone from the bureau was definitely feeding her information. Could the pilots have radioed back to FBI Headquarters and told Michelson or St. Clair? As far as I knew, only Kelly and I knew we were meeting Sterling and Tiffany at gate 47. Yet Coco Nimburu was there, too.

"She's here, Kelly. Stay close to me. She could be anyone."

"I know," Kelly said nervously.

We approached Sterling and Tiffany with caution. I was watching everyone, looking for Coco's eyes. She wasn't going to get him. Not this time. I would see to it. I flashed my credentials and said, "Come with us. The Assassin is here."

Tiffany said, "How do we know you're really FBI?"

"Ma'am, you're going to have to trust me," I told her.

"That's not good enough," Sterling said, as he bent over to set his luggage on the floor.

I heard the shuriken whistle through the air just before it found its way into Tiffany's head. Just for an instant, her eyes registered surprise before she fell to the floor. Deafening screams and shrieks filled the air. Kelly tackled Sterling like she was an NFL linebacker. I pulled my 9-millimeter. People were running in all directions. I searched for Coco, but I think she had blended in with the fleeing crowd, running and screaming like everybody else.

CHAPTER 51

W E RUSHED STERLING to the airport security office and gave him a chance to gain some perspective. I watched the wheels in his mind churn as the realization that he had just barely escaped death flooded his consciousness. I wondered if a near-death experience would be enough to override his commitment to attorney-client privilege.

Kelly set a cup of coffee in front of him. He thanked her and picked up the cup. His hands shook uncontrollably. Fear dominated his mind, I could tell. I've seen the look of sheer terror before.

"If Daunte King hadn't been in jail," Sterling finally said, "I would be negotiating with the Denver brass right now. And Tiffany would be alive."

Kelly sat across the table from Sterling and asked, "Can you tell us anything at all about the rich woman who's trying to have you killed?"

"I can't tell you anything about her. But I can tell you how to contact someone who can help you find out who she is. That's all I can do."

"Who?" I asked eagerly.

He reached for his wallet and looked through it. Then he pulled out a card and slid it across the table. I picked it up and read the name. It was Winston Keyes, and it had his telephone number on the card. I looked at Kelly and showed her the card. We smiled and gave each other high-fives.

"What?" Sterling asked. "You know Winston?"

"Not personally. But we hope to make his acquaintance soon. Real soon," I said. "So, how do you know this man?"

"He's the contact I used if I needed to speak with my client. I call that number, and he gives her the message."

"So who is Winston Keyes to the rich woman?" Kelly asked. "Are they fucking or what?"

"I wondered the same thing when I met them," Sterling said, and managed to laugh a little. Then he turned serious again. "Winston Keyes knows everything. He's not my client; she is. I don't know much about him, but I know he works for her. And I know they've been together for some time now. So yes, they're fucking."

My cell rang. "Agent Perry."

"Good work, Agent Perry," I heard Coco Nimburu say in Cantonese.

I looked at Kelly and mouthed, "It's her."

"Mr. Wise was truly lucky today. If he had not bent over to set his suitcase down, he would be explaining his sins to God right now." Coco laughed. "I was about to try again, but you were in the way. I need you alive."

"Am I supposed to thank you?"

"You should. It would be so easy to take you out. Or maybe the pretty blonde. Kelly is her name, isn't it? I could have taken her, too, but I didn't."

I looked at my best friend. I was scared for her. Coco was right. She could have killed us all and still gotten away. Airport security would have been no match for her.

"What do you want?" I said forcefully. "I've got him now. You might as well stop the killing. He knows who your client is. And he's agreed to tell us everything," I bluffed.

Coco laughed. "You're not a very good liar, Phoenix. If that were so, you wouldn't have to say it. And I know Attorney Wise wouldn't violate attorney-client privilege."

"Then what is it you want? Why did you call?"

"Just thought you should know: Cynthia Charles is dead."

"Who is Cynthia Charles?"

"Ask Mr. Wise. In the meantime, send the coroner over to 6119 Pikes Peak Boulevard. There's a stiff over there getting ripe. Ciao."

I hit the end button on the cell and turned to Sterling. He looked worried. "Is she all right? Is Cynthia okay?"

"I'm sorry to tell you, but she's dead."

"Oh no, not Cynthia, too!"

"Who was she? A girlfriend?"

"Kinda. We've known each other since my days at the Air Force Academy."

"Did you tell her anything about your client?"

"No. Nothing at all."

"The rich woman must think you did or could have."

"If that's true, you better get some people to Manhattan and Chicago. I have girlfriends there also—Crystal James in Chicago and Chase Davenport in Manhattan."

"Would you be willing to call Winston and make an appointment with your client?" Kelly asked.

"Are you kidding? Why the fuck would I do some dumb shit like that? There's a high-priced assassin out there trying to kill me. She's already killed my assistant, the Warren family, and a bunch of FBI agents. You muthafuckas can't even protect yourselves. How in the hell are you going to protect me? The goddamned assassin is calling the FBI and telling you who's dead. And you want me to stick my neck into the guillotine? You must be outta your goddamned mind."

Sterling had a point. We couldn't protect him by ourselves. We needed an army for that task.

"Let me ask you something, Agent Perry," Sterling continued. "Why is she calling you? And for that matter, how did she get your phone number? I trust you didn't give it to her, right? So that must mean someone in the FBI is giving her information. And knowing my client, it's someone at the top. Tell me you've figured that much out. That way, I might have a chance to get out of this airport in one piece."

I ignored the insult. Sterling could still tell us some things we didn't know about his client. "Why would you say that it's somebody at the top?"

"Because that's how I met her. She had a dossier on my whole family. I sat in her limo, and she read my entire history to me. That's how she knew about Cynthia. She knows about Chase and Crystal, too. Please, put some people on them before it's too late."

Sterling gave us the addresses of the women, and Kelly made calls to the

Manhattan and Chicago field offices. Beating Coco to Sterling Wise was a huge coup for Kelly and me. I was finally starting to believe we could solve this thing.

"Now that I've done something for you, Sterling, do something for me. Make the call to Winston Keyes. I'll do everything in my power to protect you."

"Yeah, like you protected the Warrens?"

"I wasn't there for that," I said, pleading my case. Truth be told, I couldn't have done much better than Ford and Flynn. "What chance do you have on your own?"

"I won't be on my own. I'll visit my brother in the Caymans. He and his wife can protect me better than the FBI can. Plus, she's a good cook. Makes all kinds of Vietnamese dishes."

Suddenly, I remembered what Coco had said about the couple at my father's funeral, a black man and a Vietnamese woman. "I think your brother was at my father's funeral. How would your brother know my father?"

"I don't know," Sterling said. "What did your father do for a living?"

"We own an investigative firm."

"That's it. I told my brother about the dossier my client had on the family when I visited him a couple of years ago. He made a call to the States and was faxed information on my client. I assume the person sending him the information was your father or someone at his firm."

I wondered if that's what Coco meant about my father not being innocent. Did he bring his own untimely death on himself? Coco had said that he knew someone would come to kill him. Were his hands dirty after all? The mystery surrounding this case was beginning to unravel, and I didn't like what I was learning. My dad was one of the good guys. How could he be involved in this sort of thing? He was always a man of integrity and principle. Maybe Coco Nimburu was right. Maybe none of us were innocent.

CHAPTER 52

STERLING WISE FLEW to the Caymans. Before he left, he told us he would be staying at the Renegade Hotel and Casino, which his brother Jericho owned. Kelly and I got back on the Director's jet and flew to Washington. On the way home, we tried to figure out who the inside man in the bureau was. Based on what Sterling had told us, it had to be either St. Clair or Michelson. St. Clair had told Michelson to take us off the case. Michelson, being the sycophant that he was, did whatever St. Clair told him.

Michelson was good at pretending to give orders when, in truth, it was St. Clair all along. The Director liked the appearance of getting along with the troops, but behind closed doors, he was a viper—worse than Michelson. He must have wanted Flynn and Ford in San Francisco, believing Coco would have a better chance with them in charge. I didn't trust either one of them. However, I had a hard time believing that agents were involved. If they were, perhaps that's why they were killed.

If anybody but Agent James had been protecting Keyth and Savannah, I would have been worried. I called the safe house from the jet, just to be sure they were okay. James assured me they were.

The first thing I wanted to do when we got back to the office was view the hotel videotapes. I thought there might be something there. Kelly and I were on our way to the evidence facility when we saw St. Clair. He didn't look happy.

"Perry, McPherson, I wanna see you in my office right now!" St. Clair shouted.

"Sir, we were just about to go over some crucial evidence that might tell us something about the Assassin," I said.

"Right now, Special Agent Perry," he barked. His determination to prevent us from going into the evidence facility cinched it for us. What was it that he didn't want us to see? We rode the elevator in silence. St. Clair waited until we got into his office and closed the door.

"What happened in San Francisco?" he demanded.

"You tell me, sir," I said with rancor. St. Clair looked confused, as if he didn't know what I was talking about. "How is it that the Assassin knew where we were staying? How is it that she knows my cell number?"

"What are you saying? You think someone is feeding her information?" he asked incredulously.

Kelly and I stared at him.

"You two think I'm feeding her information? Me?"

"Either you or Michelson," I said boldly. "Sir, twelve agents have been killed. The Assassin is good, but she's getting a lot of help. If you're not helping her, it's gotta be Michelson."

"Well, I assure you it isn't me."

"Prove it. Let me and Kelly go over the videotapes. There could be something there."

"You agree with this, Agent McPherson?"

"Yes, sir. One hundred percent."

"Okay, you two better be right about Michelson. Your jobs are on the line. Check the tapes out, and let me know what you find."

CHAPTER 53

THE EVIDENCE ROOM was secure. To enter, all personnel had to sign in and out. I looked at the register. Michelson had gone to the evidence room right after we left for San Francisco. That didn't prove anything by itself. He could have gone in there for any number of reasons. But I knew he was the informant. Kelly and I pulled the Hyatt Regency videotapes. We saw the Assassin going in and out of room 1619 wearing several disguises, all of them flawless.

I wanted to see what she did when she left the room the day we chased her. We found the tape and watched her leave the room wearing the De Matteo disguise. She went to the stairs, but there were no cameras in the stairwell. We put in tape after tape of each floor and saw her going into a room on the twentieth floor. I called the Hyatt Regency immediately to find out what name she had used. The room was registered to Debbie Morgan, another Hollywood actress.

We continued viewing the tapes, hoping to spot Michelson. We saw him enter the hotel after he chewed us out and took us off the case. From there, he took the elevator up to the sixteenth floor and went to room 1619. Then Michelson, Flynn, and Ford came out of 1619 and walked to the elevator. Michelson got on and the tape ran out. The tape of the lobby showed Michelson getting off the elevator two hours later. We searched for other tapes that might have shown us where he went, but those tapes were missing. It didn't matter though. We had enough to bring him in for questioning.

I called Michelson's secretary. "Where's Assistant Director Michelson now?" I asked.

"He called in sick," she said.

I thought it best not to say anything to St. Clair until we knew something for sure. Kelly and I went over to Michelson's house. We knocked on the door, and it swung open. With our weapons drawn, we entered cautiously. The house was frighteningly quiet. We searched the first floor, then went upstairs. Somehow, I knew Michelson was dead. It made sense. Coco was thorough. If he was in on the murders as I suspected, he had to be eliminated to protect the client. I opened the bedroom door and saw Michelson. He was naked and tied to the bed, and his neck had been snapped. Coco had left me another note in Cantonese:

Too late again, Phoenix. You can relax for a while. I am looking for the Rapist as promised. It won't be hard to find him. As I said, everything you need to know is right in front of you. I am an honest woman, and I keep my word. I will find him and kill him. In the meantime, take the time to smell the roses. You only have one life to live. Live it to the fullest.

See you soon,

Coco

CHAPTER 54

THE DEATH of Michelson was a big blow to the investigation. I called agent James and had him move my family to another house. For all I knew, Michelson had told Coco where they were. He was the link and perhaps our best chance at finding the mystery woman. At least the leak was plugged.

St. Clair decided to cover up Michelson's involvement with the Assassin, and I agreed with the decision. The bureau couldn't take another black eye right now.

For all its faults, the bureau was the nation's best crime fighting unit. I believed in what Hoover had tried to build.

Sure we had some bad apples in the bureau and some trouble in the crime lab, and a lot of unnecessary bureaucracy to deal with, but overall, we were an excellent organization, with excellent agents doing the best we could. I wasn't going to allow the fall of Michelson to tarnish the bureau. The bureau would survive his treachery and go on fighting crime.

Kelly wanted to have Sterling call Winston, but I disagreed. Calling him now would give them the advantage. We would end up tipping our hand, and we still wouldn't know what was going on. Instead, I suggested that we go back to the beginning. The bureau had done a background investigation on Judge Taylor for her nomination. I thought that would be the best place to start. I pulled her file to see if there was anything in there that would give me a clue to who she was and what she knew about the mystery woman.

Judge Taylor was the younger of two sisters. Adrienne was the elder. Her maiden name was Jefferson. She had grown up in Harlem. Then she went to Penn State University on an academic scholarship. After graduating from law school, she went on to become a civil rights attorney. In 1975, she moved to Washington, where she met and married Webster Taylor. Webster had built quite a reputation as a defense lawyer, one of the country's best. They had three children and moved to Alexandria in 1982. Five years later, she became a Fourth Circuit Court judge.

Senator Martha Blevins' story was similar to Judge Taylor's. She, too, was the younger of two siblings. Her maiden name was Bellamy, and she had grown up in privileged circumstances in Wilmington, Delaware, one of the richest communities in America. Her older brother, Jason, now deceased, had inherited the family businesses and created others.

There wasn't much in the files on either of the two women. I felt even more frustrated, and I kept thinking, I'm missing something here. Kelly and I read and reread their files, but found nothing helpful. I was ready to go home, but no one was there. I didn't dare go to the safe house, just in case Coco was lying. I didn't think she was, but can you really trust someone who kills people for money? I certainly don't.

CHAPTER 55

FATHER REYNOLDS came out of St. Mary's Cathedral at 6:00 p.m. and walked across the courtyard to the house the church provided for him. He had been busy at the church all day, catching up on his paperwork. Coco was waiting for him in the living room of the rectory. She was sitting in the priest's reading chair with her legs crossed.

"Welcome home, honey," Coco said, pointing her silenced Makarov at him. Father Reynolds stood in the doorway, astonished to see someone in his private dwelling. "Close the door," she commanded. "I don't want the neighbors to see what I'm going to do to you."

Reynolds closed the door.

"Lock it. I don't want to be interrupted either," Coco ordered.

"Young lady," Reynolds finally said, keeping his fear under control, "though your sins are many, Christ can make you whole again."

"Sit down, Father. I have some questions for you. I'm an honest woman. Tell me what I want to know, and I'll let you live. Give me a hard time, and I'll have to make you violate your vow of celibacy."

"Mary Magdalene was also a woman who had many sins. Yet, she was forgiven. Ever read the Bible?"

"Many times. Have you?" Coco said contemptuously. "Let me ask you something that has always puzzled me, Father. Where in the Bible does it say that priests have to be celibate?"

"Is that why you came here?" he asked, avoiding the question.

"You ever had a woman, Merle?" Coco asked, spreading her legs. She was wearing a short skirt outfit and no panties underneath.

He looked between her legs. "No. I've never been with a woman."

"A celibate man wouldn't look at my crotch that way, Father. Haven't you ever longed to be inside a woman? Don't you want to know what it's like to make love?"

"Every man has his cross to bear. But that's what sacrifice is all about. I willingly gave up that part of my life to serve God."

"Yes, but is that required of you? Even Peter had a wife. Why not take a wife and enjoy the pleasures of the flesh? God did make woman, did he not? And if so, she was made to be enjoyed, was she not? Yet you sacrifice one of the greatest gifts for nothing."

"What's your name, my child?"

"I am Coco Nimburu of the Nimburu clan."

"Would you like me to hear your confession?"

"Yes, and I will hear yours. It will hurt like hell, but I swear, I'll give you pleasure like you've never known before I leave." She pointed the Makarov at him. "Let's go to the bedroom, Merle. I think you'll be more comfortable there."

CHAPTER 56

I WAS CONVINCED that there was a connection between Judge Taylor and Senator Blevins. According to Coco, Taylor's murder was merciful and Blevins' murder was brutal for personal reasons. What was the common connection? I was growing more and more frustrated. I knew the answer had to be right in front of me, but I couldn't see it.

On the way home, the traffic was so heavy that I picked up the files again as I waited for the traffic lights to change. There had to be something in these records that would lead me to the mystery woman.

I reread the Blevins file. Suddenly it occurred to me that Jason Bellamy had inherited most of the family money. Did he leave the money to Martha when he died? Money was always a motive for murder. I flipped the page to see how Jason had died, hoping that would tell me something. But it turned out that he had died of a heart attack. But I still wanted to know where the money had gone. The Blevins certainly weren't hurting for money, judging by the size of their elegant house. What's missing? I asked myself. PICTURES!

There were no photographs of either sibling in their files. I wondered why. Did Michelson remove them? Probably so. But why? What possible difference could the pictures of siblings make? It had to make a difference, probably a big one. There were pictures of both the Taylor and the Blevins families, but no pictures of Jason or Adrienne. Why? I called Kelly and told her I was going to the Taylor house to look for pictures of Adrienne. She growled a little but promised to go to the Blevins' house to check for photos of Jason. It could be nothing, but we had to follow every clue.

CHAPTER 57

THE PRIEST was naked and tied to the bed. Six golden needles were strategically placed in his chest to produce the stiff penis. Father Reynolds still had no idea what this woman wanted.

"I need to know everything you know about the Rapist," Coco said.

"I can't tell you anything. I'm a priest, for God's sake. Please...don't do this."

"I have to. I made a promise. I know you know something. What did he tell you?"

Reynolds was quiet.

"Okay, I gave you fair warning." She put a gag in his mouth, then pulled out a set of silver needles. "Merle, are you sure you want to go through this? Tell me what I want to know."

Reynolds shook his head.

Coco picked up a needle and inserted it into his right testicle. The pain was excruciating, but the gag muffled the priest's screams. Coco pulled the needle out and the pain stopped. "You ready to tell me now, Merle? Why go through all of this? You're going to tell me everything eventually."

Reynolds shook his head again.

She reinserted the needle. "I'll be right back. I'm going to make a pot of tea. I can see this is going to take a while." She left the room humming "Onward Christian Soldiers."

She found an old-fashioned teakettle in the pantry and let cold water from the faucet run into its spout. When the water was ready, the kettle would whistle. She reached into the cookie jar and took out some Oreos. When she went back into the bedroom, sweat was pouring off Father Reynolds, the pain was so great. Coco sat on the bed—expressionless.

"That's just one needle, Merle," she said and ate a cookie. "I feel it's important that I tell you that if I insert all six needles, you will die. Now, do you really want that?"

Reynolds shook his head. Coco stared into his eyes. She wanted him to be aware of her personal resolve. He needed to see that she could administer pain without emotion or remorse. She put another cookie in her mouth; then she pulled the needle out.

"Better?"

He nodded.

"Are you ready to talk to me?"

Reynolds shook his head. Coco ate another cookie and shrugged her shoulders. Then she reinserted the first needle and stuck in two more. Reynolds' muffled screams were more anguished than before. "If you were ever going to have children, I would worry about having that many needles in one testicle. But since you're not ever going to be having any, there's no need to be concerned."

She picked up the remote control and turned on the television. *Entertainment Tonight* was on. "You ever watch this show, Merle? It gives you all the dirt on the celebrities." The teapot whistled. "Be right back," she said, and hopped off the bed.

CHAPTER 58

THE TAYLOR HOUSE was just as we had left it. I wondered what the children were going to do with it. It was such a nice place. I walked into the living room, looking for family portraits. I saw dozens of them but none of Adrienne, not that I could tell anyway. There were pictures of Webster and Jennifer and their children, but not many of anyone else. I saw several pictures of two young black couples. I assumed they were the parents of Webster and Jennifer.

It was truly strange not to see any pictures of Adrienne in the house. Maybe the sisters weren't on speaking terms. Maybe Adrienne was dead, and the memory of her sister was too painful for Jennifer. But that didn't explain why there weren't any pictures of her in the file. Even if she were dead, what difference did it make? On the other hand, there was nothing in the file that said Adrienne was dead while the Blevins file had information that Jason was dead. I was really curious now. Jason was dead, Adrienne probably wasn't, but there were no pictures of either. I was onto something. I could feel it.

Did Michelson remove the pictures? Where would Judge Taylor keep any family pictures that she didn't want seen? I went into the master bedroom. A lot of women have a special drawer where they hide their keepsakes. If I could find her keepsakes, I might find pictures of Adrienne, I thought. I wasn't sure why I was determined to find pictures of her, but they were missing from the file, and my heart told me they were important.

I opened all the drawers, searched the armoire, and looked under the bed. Nothing. Frustration was beginning to mount again. I knew there must have been keepsakes somewhere; it was just a matter of finding them. I went into Jennifer Taylor's huge walk-in closet. There were several boxes stacked on the shelves. I took a deep breath and blew it out.

This was going to take forever. It occurred to me that even after spending twelve years in a Shaolin Temple, I still lacked sufficient patience. Master Ying Ming Lo had been on me constantly about that. Someday, I would master patience.

CHAPTER 59

IPPING HER TEA, Coco watched television and ate more Oreo cookies. Father Reynolds' muffled screams and constant squirming didn't bother her. From time to time, she would check to see if he was ready to talk. He had five needles in him now—the most she had ever inserted. She admired his high threshold for pain. She took the last swallow of her tea and looked at Reynolds.

It was almost 8:30; he had been holding out for more than two hours. Coco turned off the TV with the remote control and positioned herself between his legs. She shook the needles back and forth, forcing them in deeper. The priest's body was gyrating up and down.

"You ready to talk to me now?" Coco asked patiently. He nodded. Tears were running down his rose-colored cheeks. Coco pulled the needles out and he was able to relax a little. His chest moved up and down rapidly. After removing the gag, she asked, "Do you know his name?"

"No."

"Have you seen him since the rape?"

"Yes. He comes to confession once, sometimes twice a week."

"When will he come again?"

"Tomorrow morning. He comes in on his lunch hour, right around noon."

"See, that wasn't too hard, was it? Here, have an Oreo. They're delicious." He opened his mouth and she put a cookie in. "You ready for phase two? You're gonna love this."

Father Reynolds' eyes enlarged when Coco took off her clothes. "What are you doing? I told you everything! Don't do this!" he pleaded.

"Relax, Father. I'm going to take good care of you."

He struggled as best he could but it did no good. Coco laughed uproariously. "Don't fight it, Father. You might as well relax and enjoy it. This is going to happen."

The more he struggled, the more it turned Coco on. Now, she had him. And it felt good. She began slowly. When the priest was no longer struggling, her thrusts became more powerful and rapid. Father Reynolds' eyes rolled back into his head—only the whites were visible.

"See what you've been missing, Father?"

He didn't answer, but he was moving with her now. Her rhythm was fast and furious, but he kept up. Two hours later, Father Reynolds was still going strong, but Coco had had enough.

"I need to stop for a while," she told him as she stretched out next to him. "Give me half an hour. We've got all night and tomorrow, at least until the Rapist shows up."

CHAPTER 60

I TOOK THE FIRST BOX off the shelf and opened it. It was full of cards and letters from Webster. Kelly and I had been too busy to be thorough at the time of the assassinations. This time, I would be meticulous. I got to the bottom of the box, but there were no pictures in it. Undeterred, I carefully put everything back in the box the way I had found it and opened the next box. My cell rang. It was Kelly. Maybe she was having better luck.

"Hi, Kelly. You find anything?"

"Yeah. Did you?"

"Not yet. What did you find?"

"I got some pictures of the family. They were in the basement."

"Is that where you started?"

"No, I started in the bedroom. That's where I keep my stuff."

"Me, too. Judge Taylor's got an entire box dedicated to all the cards, letters, and notes from flowers her husband sent her over the past twenty-five years."

"Wow! They were the real thing, huh?"

"Yeah. Makes me more determined to find out who paid Coco Nimburu to do this to them and why. Bring the pictures over. Hopefully, by the time you get here, I'll have something also."

"I'm on my way."

I opened the next box. It was full of their children's nostalgia, everything from birth certificates to baby shoes to school report cards to high school diplomas and yearbooks. No pictures in this box, either. I started to wonder if I should go to the basement and see what was down there. This was looking like a dead end. I opened the next box and still nothing. I had three more boxes to go.

Starving for some good news, I called the safe house to talk to my husband. It was nine o'clock; Savannah should be ready for bed now. I hadn't talked to her in a few days. That was unusual for me. Keyth came to the telephone.

"Hi, baby. Where are you? I called the hotel and they said you had checked out without staying the night."

"Yeah, I got a call from the Assassin. Would you believe she was in the same hotel as us?"

"Why didn't you check the register when you checked in?"

"Keyth, they've got a million hotels in San Francisco. How was I to know she was going to be at the same hotel I was in?"

He was quiet.

"What Keyth? Don't hold back. Let's hear it. How was I supposed to know she was going to be at the same hotel I was in?"

"Because you're the special agent in charge. It's your job to know. You should have at least checked."

"Well, thank you very much, Keyth. Thanks for making me feel so damn good about myself."

"You're welcome," he said flippantly. "You can get mad at me if you want to, but you should have known to check that first. You didn't and now you have the nerve to blame me for how you feel? When we were in the Islands, weren't you the one who had the theory that the assassin had gone back to the Hyatt? And if that's true, seems like you would have checked with the desk clerk when you checked in, seeing that it would have been very convenient."

"You know, Keyth. I don't even want to talk to you anymore tonight. Is Savannah still up?"

"Yeah. Hold on."

"Hi, Mommy," I heard my daughter say.

"Hi, precious. And how are you?"

"Fine. You and Daddy mad at each other, huh?"

"Just a little."

"Why, 'cause you didn't check the hotel first?" I didn't say anything. "Mommy, why didn't you check the hotel first?"

"It's time for you to go to bed. Put your daddy back on the phone," I said, growing angrier at their repeated questions. Keyth came back to the telephone. "Did you put her up to that?"

"No. She must have overheard me discussing it with you."

"Well, you know what, Keyth? Thank you for a pleasant conversation. GOOD NIGHT!" I shouted and hit the end button.

I could hear Kelly's Stingray pull into the driveway. At least it wouldn't be a totally wasted night. She had found something already. With her helping at the Taylor house, I hoped we could find some pictures of Adrienne more quickly.

PART 3
PRETENSES

CHAPTER 61

KELLY STARTED in the basement, and I continued looking through the boxes in the closet. She hadn't been down there twenty minutes, when I heard her yell, "EUREKA!" It had been a rough night; I hadn't found anything and Kelly was becoming a regular Indiana Jones. Oh, well, I thought, at least we got something.

Kelly brought in an old projector, a screen, and several reels. I assumed the reels would contain something on the family. While Kelly set up the projector, I continued looking through the last box. I found a picture of Judge Taylor and a white girl. They were standing in front of a corner deli in Harlem, dressed in skirts and knee-high socks. I turned the picture over and read: Jennifer and Adrienne Jefferson, ages 6 and 8. I was floored.

Then it all came to me at once. Images from the Four Seasons flooded my mind. I understood now. The Judge was arguing with her sister in that suite. But why? Then I began to think the unimaginable. Did Adrienne have her sister killed? If so, why?

"Kelly, you better take a look at this."

"What?" I handed her the picture. "Adrienne is Jennifer's sister?"

"Apparently. You know what that means, don't you?" I asked.

"The white woman at the Four Seasons is this little girl?"

"Yep."

"Oh, my God. Then that means Judge Taylor's own sister could have had her killed. But why?"

"I don't know. Let's keep digging," I said, with renewed vigor. "Who knows what else we're going to unearth."

As I continued searching the box, I found more pictures of Adrienne and Jennifer. They were both beautiful women. I saw the pictures of whom I presumed were their parents. I wasn't sure, so I went to the living room and looked at the black couples on the wall. Removing the photo from one of the frames, I was able to see the names of their parents written on the back. Thomas and Vivian Jefferson, it read. Although I now knew she and Jennifer were sisters, I found it hard to believe that Adrienne was black. She had blonde hair, blue eyes, and a Nordic nose.

I went back in the bedroom, still puzzled by the difference in the physical characteristics of the two sisters. Maybe Vivian had had an affair with a white man. That would explain the differences. But it would also mean that Thomas would have had to have known about it. Or maybe she had a relationship with a white man before she even met Thomas, and he had accepted mother and daughter. That was plausible, too.

Kelly finally got the old projector to work, and we watched old family movies for about an hour. We learned quite a bit. Thomas married Vivian when Adrienne was a baby. Apparently, she had a relationship with a white man during the Harlem Renaissance. That sort of thing was widespread at the time. But it still left many unanswered questions. For example, if Adrienne was behind the killings, what could possibly be her motive? Sterling Wise knew but refused to say.

After we finished watching the home movies, Kelly took the projector back to the basement while I went through the last box. I found some pictures of Adrienne's wedding to a white man. It was Jason Bellamy. Kelly came back into the room. I showed her the picture.

"I think we hit the mother lode, Phoenix." She beamed.

"Kelly, if you were black but looked white, would you hide your identity and live among whites? Or would you stay with blacks?"

"Tough question, Phoenix. You know I'm not racist, but at the same time, there are privileges and advantages to being white. For example, do you think she could have married Bellamy if she looked more like Jennifer, who was darker and had more African features?"

"Probably not," I said. "Assuming that Adrienne is behind all of the killings, what's her motive?"

"Maybe she was trying to hide the fact that she was black pretending to be white?"

"Is that a reason to kill that many people?"

"Well, consider what she had to lose, Phoenix. Jason Bellamy was a billionaire. He inherited most of the Bellamy money and the businesses, which he evidently left to Adrienne. If people knew she was black pretending to be white, she might lose a lot of influence."

"True, but do you kill your own flesh and blood for that? If the world found out, she would still be a billionaire, wouldn't she?"

"I think there's something else going on, Phoenix."

"Me too, Kelly. I think that Martha Blevins probably disapproved of the marriage. According to Coco, Martha was supposed to be brutalized first, then killed."

"You ready to have Sterling give her a call?"

"We don't need him any longer. The only thing left to find out is why she did it. Let's call it a night and get some rest. Tomorrow, we find out everything there is to know about Adrienne Bellamy."

CHAPTER 62

Sex with Father Reynolds continued until the wee hours of the morning. It was the first and only sexual encounter he would ever have. As usual, Coco thought it was the least she could do. The alarm's high-pitched tone jerked her out of a deep sleep at 10:00 A.M. She opened her eyes and looked at Reynolds, who was wide-awake.

"Ready for another round, Father?" she asked, looking at his stiff shaft. She had left the golden needles in his chest all night. He nodded his head quickly several times. "Addictive, isn't it?" she asked, climbing on top of him.

After fifteen minutes of intense sex, Coco grabbed a hunk of his hair and jerked to the right, snapping his neck. Then she took a shower and put on her priest disguise. She walked into the sanctuary of the church and saw a female parishioner already at the confessional. She was about 5 feet 5 inches and athletic-looking, pretty, with chestnut hair and wearing an expensive gray bouclé jacket, offset by a burgundy mock turtleneck, matching slacks, and Italian-made burgundy shoes with clear vinyl sides. Coco laughed to herself and thought, this is going to be fun. Too bad my life is almost over.

She walked into the confessional and sat down. The first parishioner entered and waited quietly. Coco was wondering why the parishioner wasn't confessing her dirty little secrets, then realized that she hadn't slid the panel open. After opening the window, the woman said, "Bless me, Father, for I have sinned." The woman had a genteel voice, and sounded well-educated.

"How long has it been since your last confession, my child?" she said, imitating Father Reynolds' voice.

"It's been six months since my last confession."

"Go on, my child," Coco said, covering her mouth while she chuckled under her breath.

"I have sold myself to my husband's friends."

"Why have you done this?" she asked, feeling better about her own sins. "Do you need the money or what?"

"Yes. It all began when my husband lost his well-paying position at...well, I'd rather not say. But the company was downsized, and he's been out of work for a year. We have a twenty-five-hundred-dollar monthly mortgage payment, and I didn't know what we were going to do. My husband's best friend offered me the mortgage money if I would have sex with him. That's how it all started. I was desperate, Father," she said, then sniffed a couple of times.

"Go on, my child. Free yourself." Coco could barely contain the enormous glee that began to bubble to the surface, forcing her to grin widely.

"I was doing it for the money. You know, to take care of our family. At first sex with them was an arduous chore. But then, I started to like it." The woman was crying now. "Each time I committed the act, little by little, the real me began to emerge. The me that I've kept hidden deep within. The me that no one knew about. The me that has longed to be free from social restraints."

"Go on," Coco encouraged.

"I continue taking their money, but the truth is, after a while, I would have done it for nothing, Father. That's when I realized that I was a whore. I've always been a whore, if only in my mind. I found myself living out every fantasy I've ever had with these men. I'm so ashamed."

"No need to be ashamed, my child," Coco said. "Tell me, does your husband know about this?"

"I eventually told him, yes."

"Ah, the truth has set you free then?"

"Yes."

"Are you still seeing the men, my child?"

"Yes."

"What are you charging them?"

"Just what it costs to survive. We have three children in very expensive private schools. Twenty-five hundred dollars each—no more."

"Raise your price to four thousand dollars. Or increase the number of times you see them per month. I'm sure you have needs and desires, judging by that expensive outfit you're wearing. And if they pay that sum, continue the practice, but make sure you come to confession. If they refuse to pay, tell their wives. Now, go in peace, my child."

When the woman left the confessional, Coco laughed so hard she could hardly sit still. She composed herself when the next parishioner entered.

The next seven or eight parishioners' confessions were boring compared to the first woman. Coco began to wonder how long it would be before the Rapist arrived. Anxious to meet him, she hoped he would be on time.

"Bless me, Father, for I have sinned."

"How long has it been since your last confession, my son?"

"About a week."

"Go on, my son? Unburden yourself."

"Father, I murdered a woman."

Coco suddenly became serious. She wondered if this was the Rapist. She looked at her watch. It was only eleven. It was a little early for the Rapist, according to the time that Father Reynolds told her. He shouldn't have been there for another hour.

"Go on, my son. Why did you murder the woman?"

"As you know, I haven't been able to control my urge to rape men." Coco raised her eyebrows. It was the Rapist. She was a little disappointed she wasn't going to be able to hear more confessions. After the first one, she was hooked.

"I followed them through Union Station. They looked like the perfect couple. I thought he loved her and would fight to keep her from being raped. Apparently, he didn't care for her at all. The two of them ended up in a big fight. When I tried to break them up, he grabbed the gun and it went off. It was an accident. The whole scene was bizarre. I knew I had to kill her, but the strange thing is I feel so liberated now. Don't get me wrong, Father, I felt bad for a few days, but I got over it. Given enough time, you can get over anything."

"Tell me, my son, will you stop violating men, now that you've committed murder?"

"No. I'm even more committed to doing it. Isn't that strange, Father? After you forgave me, my mind was made up. I was going to stop. But after a few days, the desire to do it again was stronger than it had ever been. After the murder, I felt terrible, but now I feel like I've been emancipated, like the burden of morality has been eradicated. I don't think I'm ever coming to see you again," he said, then abruptly left the confessional.

CHAPTER 63

T HE NUMBER that Sterling had given us for Winston Keyes turned out to be an office in the World Trade Center. Apparently, Adrienne Bellamy kept a business office there. According to the computer-generated voice mail, Winston Keyes would return our call if we left a message. I wasn't ready to meet with Bellamy just yet. I wanted to learn as much about her as I could.

I ran her name through the bureau's computers and learned that she had part ownership in several sports franchises. Shortly before his death, Jason Bellamy had launched a new, commercially sponsored television network. When Adrienne took over, she landed a professional football contract, which catapulted the network to the fourth largest, behind NBC, ABC, and CBS. The football contract opened many other doors, and before long, her network was producing Emmy-winning dramas and situation comedies.

She also held large quantities of stock in the major film studios in Hollywood and Burbank. Her assets included full ownership of three major newspapers, a chain of grocery stores, department stores, movie theaters, several malls, a shipyard, and a Las Vegas casino. The litany of enterprises she had her hands in went on and on. I was impressed and intimidated at the same time, but she had broken the law. Everything we learned indicated that she had been responsible for the killing of her own flesh and blood, several of Washington's elite, and a dozen FBI agents. I had to bring her down.

CHAPTER 64

THE RAPIST was a handsome man, Coco thought, tall, slim, and well-muscled. She was following him in a rented Intrepid, still dressed as the priest. The ninja motorcycle would have brought too much unnecessary attention. The Rapist went to Union Station, bought a paper, and sat at an empty table in the middle of the food court. Tourists from all over the world occupied the busy concourse.

Coco filled a huge salad bowl with lettuce, tomatoes, onions, cheese, peppers, turkey, ham, and bacon bits, topped with bleu cheese, and Thousand Island dressing. She paid the vendor for the salad and picked up a bottle of Arizona Tea.

From a table near the Rapist, she watched his every move without appearing to. While she ate her salad, she read the Washington Post someone had left at her table. When she looked up again, she saw Phoenix Perry and Kelly McPherson coming into the food court.

Coco's eyes darted left and right, seeking the quickest way to escape. There wasn't a nearby exit, but there were plenty of people. If necessary, she would grab the nearest child and shoot her way out. Coco could feel her anger building. Phoenix was ruining everything. She had tracked down the Rapist. He was hers to kill, not Phoenix's. This was her time—her show. She pulled two shuriken from her vest, preparing to throw them if necessary. Then the strangest thing happened. Phoenix and Kelly went to the Rapist's table and sat down. McPherson kissed him.

CHAPTER 65

THIS WAS FUN. Apparently, Kelly McPherson and the Rapist had a personal relationship. Coco continued eating her salad, planning her next move. She was still going to kill the man. It would just take a little longer, but she was patient. After an hour or so, the trio left the food court. Kelly rode with the Rapist, and Phoenix drove off in her Mustang Cobra. This was working out beautifully, Coco thought. She was going to get rid of Kelly anyway, and this was the perfect opportunity.

Coco followed the couple to Arlington, where they went to the Hyatt Regency Hotel on Wilson Boulevard. Coco chuckled when people stared at her and mumbled about a priest in the hotel. If they only knew!

Coco took an elevator to the laundry floor, changed into a maid's uniform, and then went back to the lobby, where she picked up a white courtesy telephone. She had seen Kelly McPherson pay for the room with a credit card. Coco told the desk clerk that she had an order for McPherson but she had forgotten the room number. The desk clerk told Coco what room they were in.

She knocked on the door and yelled, "Champagne and cheese, compliments of hotel management." The Rapist opened the door slightly and Coco kicked it in, sending him spiraling across the room. Kelly went for her gun on the nightstand. A shuriken whistled through the air and slammed into the wood, just missing her hand.

"WHAT THE HELL IS THIS?" the Rapist yelled.

"Simon, it's the Assassin," Kelly said with resignation.

Coco closed the door gently, watching Simon, who had on nothing but a towel. She looked at Kelly. "You two crazy kids havin' fun on taxpayers' money? For shame."

She pulled out her silenced Makarov and pointed at Simon. "On your feet," she ordered. Simon stood up. "Drop the towel. Let's see what you've got to offer." Simon did as she directed. Coco looked at his tool. "Not bad, Kelly. But what would you say if I told you he was sticking it in men?"

Kelly frowned. "What are you talking about?"

Simon was about to go for the gun. Coco squeezed off a shot. Simon screamed and fell to his knees. The bullet had blown off his manhood. Thick blood covered his hands as he held what was left of his valued organ.

"You mean you didn't know that your boyfriend was the Rapist?"

"That's impossible!" Kelly shouted, unable to accept the truth.

"Oh, really? He confessed to me this morning at Father Reynolds' church," Coco revealed.

"No way!" Simon groaned. "Don't believe her, Kelly! The bitch is lying!"

Coco looked down at him. "I was in the confessional, you idiot! Remember the priest in Union Station, Kelly? You looked right at me."

The wheels in Kelly's mind started to turn. Then a look of total disgust appeared on her face. She knew Coco was telling the truth. Kelly covered her mouth and ran to the bathroom, leaned over the toilet, and vomited.

Coco laughed. "It's sickening, isn't it?" She saw a wallet on the nightstand and picked it up. "Let's see who you are, Mister Rapist." She saw Simon's D.C. detective's shield and laughed. "I might get into heaven after all."

Kelly looked like a ghost when she came out of the bathroom. She was still stunned by the revelation. "Put your clothes on, Agent McPherson. You don't want people to find you in the raw, do you? Don't worry; I'm not going to kill you. I'm going to be merciful. Phoenix is going to need a friend when this is all over. Consider yourself lucky."

"What about me? If you get me to the hospital now, they can sew it back on. I'll be all right," Simon pleaded.

"You're not going to need it anymore," Coco told him. The Makarov hissed twice and two bullets entered Simon's head, killing him instantly. She turned to Kelly and said, "I gotta put you outta commission for a while. This is between me and Phoenix now."

CHAPTER 66

PHOENIX PERRY went to the safe house and knocked on the door. Agent James looked through the peephole and yelled, "What's the authorization code?"

"Alpha and Omega. The beginning and the end."

"Just checking to make sure it was you, Agent Perry," James said, opening the door.

Coco Nimburu pulled her silenced Makarov, pumped two shots into his forehead, and he fell to the floor. Three more agents sitting at a card table went for their weapons, but it was too late. She shot them all. There was no sign of Keyth and Savannah. She pulled the expensive mask off and searched the house. The bathroom door was locked, and she heard the shower running. She assumed it was Keyth.

"Hi," she heard Savannah say.

Coco put the gun behind her back and knelt on one knee. "You must be Savannah."

"Uh-huh. What's your name?"

"Coco. Where's your daddy?"

"He takin' a shower. Mommy's coming over later."

"I'm here to take you on a special trip. Go get your things together, okay, sweetheart?"

Savannah ran to her room. Coco couldn't hear the shower running anymore. She waited for Keyth to come out, then put the gun to the back of his head.

"Relax," Coco whispered. "I'm not going to kill you. If I were, you'd be dead already. Remember, Keyth, Savannah's in her room. Don't do anything stupid. Let's just go to your room, get your things, and go."

"I assume the agents are dead?" Keyth said calmly. He'd been an FBI agent assigned to the Criminal Division of the bureau and had seen his share of death.

Coco smiled. "It was too easy."

"Can we leave through the back door? I don't want Savannah to see that."

"If you cooperate, you'll find that I'm very easy to please. Now move."

CHAPTER 67

KELLY OPENED her eyes and saw me staring back at her. Coco had beaten her to within an inch of her life, breaking an arm and a leg. Her face was swollen from the fight. I was sure she had done her best, but she was overmatched. It was difficult to look at her without cringing. I had to be a trooper for her sake. Yet underneath my smiling exterior lay a smoldering fire burning at a thousand degrees Fahrenheit.

"How you doin', Kelly?"

"Glad to be alive," she mumbled through swollen lips. "Glad to be alive."

"I'm glad you're alive, too." I took her hand. "I'm sorry about Simon."

"I had no idea he was the Rapist, Phoenix. None at all. I feel like such an idiot. I'm an FBI agent, for Christ's sake."

"How could you have known? Some people are good at pretenses." I changed the subject. "We found Father Reynolds. His balls were purple."

"At least he went out happy," Kelly said, trying to add levity to a grim situation. "She's really something else."

"Why didn't she kill you?" I felt funny asking the question, as if I weren't glad she was alive. But I had to ask. Coco Nimburu was killing just about everyone who crossed her path. Yet Kelly was alive.

"She said you were going to need a friend when this is over. Doing this to me was her way of being merciful."

"What did she mean by that, Kelly?" Then it occurred to me. She was going after my family. I called the safe house but no one answered. "I gotta go, Kelly. She's after my family!"

CHAPTER 68

I RAN THROUGH Washington Memorial Hospital with the speed of a gazelle, worried sick about Keyth and Savannah. The spat we had had flooded my mind. I feared I would never see them again. Keyth was right. Had I checked the Embassy's registration, we might have caught Coco in San Francisco. Now, this ruthless homicidal maniac was probably going after my husband and daughter. She would stop at nothing to hurt me.

I hopped into my Cobra and burned rubber out of the parking garage. I was about to call Director St. Clair when my cell rang.

"Special Agent Perry."

"Hello, Agent Perry. I want you to speak to someone," Coco said in Cantonese.

"Hi, Mommy! Coco's taking me and Daddy to McDonald's."

My heart pounded in my chest when I heard Savannah's voice. She was still alive. I was relieved but still overwhelmed with worry. "Hi, sweetheart, let me speak to Coco, okay?"

"You've got a lot to prove, Phoenix," Coco continued in Cantonese. "I'm starting to wonder if you were ever a student of Ying Ming Lo. Now I have to see if you're worthy of what I asked of you."

"Now you listen to me, you trifling-ass bitch," I interrupted. "If you harm one hair on her head, I'll kill you."

"Now we understand each other. You just needed a little motivation, that's all. Listen very carefully. You're going to get a call from my client. She wants to meet with you, but I have plans for you first. Keep your phone with you at all times. Ciao."

CHAPTER 69

THE SAFE HOUSE door was closed but not locked. When I entered the premises, I saw Agent James lying on the floor, his eyes staring at the ceiling. Three other agents were still sitting in their chairs, slumped over the poker table. My anger was getting more and more out of control. I wanted to kill Coco Nimburu for many reasons, none of which would be ruled a justifiable homicide.

As I looked around, I saw a mask made to look just like me. Confused, I wondered why James had let Coco in. He was a by-the-book agent. I was sure he would have asked for my authorization code. I went back to the door. The door had indeed been opened from the inside. He had let her in. Why? Oh, no. She had my authorization code, too. But how? Michelson didn't know it. My phone! She had bugged my phone! I opened it, expecting to see a listening and tracking device, but there wasn't one. Then it occurred to me—somehow, she had been able to bug our hotel rooms in San Francisco. "Michelson! Damn him to hell!" I shouted.

The rest of the team arrived at the safe house and began a futile investigation. They wouldn't find anything of use. Coco Nimburu was too good. But she wasn't perfect, and that would be her undoing. Did she really have AIDS? Did she really want to die? Or was she playing another sick game? I didn't know, but I couldn't afford not to play along. The lives of my husband and daughter were at stake. Coco would call again, and this time, I would be ready for her.

Director St. Clair walked into the safe house with a grim look on his face, like he was both sad and under a lot of pressure. I understood. Coco was making us all look like idiots. She was doing whatever she wanted, killing whomever she wanted, and even having sex with whomever she wanted. I wondered if she was going to take Keyth the way she had taken so many other men in her wake.

"Perry, how do you wanna play this?" St. Clair said. "Your family's on the line."

"Sir, she's going to call again," I began. "Monitor my phone and get a Cantonese-speaking agent to interpret. That way, you'll know everything I know immediately. We'll need tracking devices on my car, phone, and clothing. She's very smart, sir. So we dare not underestimate her."

CHAPTER 70

YING MING LO had taught me many things, and I had been his best student. Now more than ever, I remembered what he had told me about my temper, but I felt so powerless against its consuming fire. With each act of violence against my family and friends, my anger burned more and more out of control. I needed to rest to give the fire a chance to subside. I would need to be in control when Coco Nimburu and I met. The waiting was extremely difficult—knowing she would call yet, not knowing when tested my patience as well. I decided to go home, take a hot bath, and meditate. A hot bath always relieved my tension, and meditation would help prepare me for battle.

I entered my house through the garage and went straight to the bathroom adjoining our bedroom. The house felt so empty, so quiet, without Keyth and Savannah. The water was hot, but it felt good. I could feel the day's stress leaving my overworked body. I was on my own now that Kelly had been skillfully put out of commission. I wondered if Kelly would ever find the right man. In the years I had known her, she had always had bad luck with men. Simon had seemed so right, which proves you never know until you know.

Before him, it was Edward, who thought of Kelly as his trophy. Then there was Tony, who was always broke and in debt up to his neck. Before him, there were Bobby, Kevin, and John, her good-for-nothing husband. Each of them had a variety of problems. I felt bad for Kelly. She was divorced with two children who spent more time with their grandparents than with their mother. At least she would have time to spend with them now, I thought.

Climbing out of the sunken tub, I grabbed a towel and dried off. I sat in front of the mirror and looked at myself. I had never realized until now how important my family was to me. They were important before but even more so now. I tried to relax but found myself getting frustrated again. I went back into the bedroom and plopped down on the bed. I felt something when I landed. Lifting myself up a little, I pulled a videotape out from underneath me. It read: *Play me.*

I put the videotape in the VCR and hit the play button. What I saw rekindled my anger with a vengeance. Coco had tied Keyth to our bed and stripped him naked. She had the needles strategically placed, giving him a permanent erection. Then I heard Coco ask, "Should we make her watch, Keyth? Or should we let her drive herself crazy wondering what I was going to do to you? Or will she wonder where Savannah is while we're in here taking care of an itch that just won't go away."

Keyth looked into the camera and closed his eyes, then shook his head. Coco laughed. "Can't bear to watch, huh, Keyth? I know what you must be going through, wondering how this is going to look with your wife knowing that as much as you tried to resist, you couldn't. And then wondering if your marriage will ever be the same after she sees you thrusting yourself inside me with reckless abandon. I just can't wait to ride you. It's so long and thick. Looks like it'll completely fill my love box. I think I'll start off with a little appetizer." I heard her smacking her lips as though she were eating something very tasty. "I wonder how much of you I can take." She smacked her lips again. The videotape became snowy.

I sat at the edge of our bed and cried, wondering if this nightmare would ever end. She had killed my father and kidnapped my husband and daughter. Now she was fucking my husband with my daughter somewhere in the house. I needed to talk to someone. Kelly was the first person who came to mind.

"Hello," Kelly mumbled through swollen lips.

CHAPTER 71

POURING OUT my soul to Kelly helped, but it didn't get rid of the images that would be forever etched in my mind. I knew it wasn't Keyth's fault, but I still blamed him. He should have fought harder or died trying, I thought. I realized I was blaming him unfairly, but I was powerless to stop myself. Coco Nimburu had gotten to me like no other person had gotten to me—ever. She was pulling my strings and, like a puppet, I did whatever the puppet master commanded. The stress that the bath had relieved was now back and in control of my waking hours.

Fortunately, I had been able to sleep after crying for about an hour. It was a new day, and maybe something good was going to happen. I needed to eat, but my appetite was gone. The sight of seeing my husband and another woman in our bedroom had caused my stomach to flip. I still felt nauseated at the memory, but I needed to press on. After showering, I turned on the television and watched The Morning Show on CBS. My cell rang.

I had left it in the bedroom, and I scrambled to get to it before it stopped ringing. "Hello," I said urgently.

"Get to Union Station immediately," Coco said in Mandarin. "I know you speak Mandarin, so don't pretend you don't. You will be given further instructions once you're there. I'll be watching your every move. I know the FBI is listening so do exactly as I tell you."

CHAPTER 72

I FELT FOOLISH. She had manipulated me again. I had told the bureau to get someone who speaks Cantonese, but Coco was speaking Mandarin now. As far as I know, I am the only agent in the Washington office that speaks that language. I'm sure Michelson gave her that inside information, too. Luckily, we had the car, the phone, and my clothes bugged. They would know where I was—even if they couldn't understand what we were saying.

I bolted out of the house and headed for Union Station. I wanted my husband back, no matter what. Keyth and I had a special relationship, and we could overcome this, I told myself. The few hours of sleep had helped give me a fresh perspective.

I parked in the garage and took the escalator down to the mall entrance. With no instructions, I wondered what I was going to do. Then I heard my name being paged, calling me to a courtesy telephone. I found the nearest telephone and said, "Agent Perry."

"Go down to the ticket booth and pick up a ticket waiting for you," Coco said in Mandarin. She was probably being cautious, just in case the bureau had found an interpreter who worked for a different agency in Washington. She couldn't afford to take any chances, I assumed, not when she was so close to getting what she wanted. "Don't call anybody. Don't get anything to eat. Don't even go to the bathroom. Get on the train and wait for further instructions."

I looked around, hoping to see an agent following me. I didn't see anyone. I went to the ticket booth and told the clerk my name. He handed me a first-class ticket to Manhattan and told me the train was just boarding. I had to run to catch it. As I climbed aboard, I looked over my shoulder. I still saw no agents and no sign of Coco Nimburu. The conductor looked at my ticket and led me to a private car near the dining section of the train. As we pulled out of the station, I looked at my watch; it was 10 a.m.

The car was luxurious and contained a well-stocked refrigerator with wine, cheese, crackers, lunchmeat, and fruit. Adrienne Bellamy had probably paid for my private car. I reached into my pocket to tip the conductor, but he told me the tip had already been taken care of.

I have to admit I liked having a private luxury car. Being rich does have its rewards, I thought. Then I heard a cell phone ringing, but it wasn't mine. I lifted the storage hatch where the ringing was coming from and found a phone.

"Hello."

"How do you like the place?" Coco asked. "Nice, huh?"

"Let me talk to my husband and daughter," I said forcefully.

"All in good time. Right now, I want you to strip."

I frowned. "What?"

"I know all about the bugs and tracking devices in clothing." She laughed. "Strip and throw everything out of the window, including your bra and panties. I just wish I could be there to see you in all your splendor. I bet I could make you purr like a kitten. You'd love it."

"What am I supposed to wear?"

"I took your black uniform and some underwear. Everything you need is in the closet."

"Okay, I'm throwing everything out now," I said, checking to see if she was on the train. If she were, Keyth and Savannah might be, too.

"You didn't throw anything out, Phoenix. Are you happy? Now you know I'm on the train. Throw everything out, including your phone, right now."

I followed her instructions to the letter. "Now what?"

"Sit back and enjoy the ride. Ciao."

CHAPTER 73

MY APPETITE returned, and I was able to eat the breakfast I had been given. It was very good. I wondered what was waiting for me in Manhattan. Then I remembered that Sterling Wise had told me that Chase Davenport lived there. She was still alive though. For some reason, Coco hadn't gone after her, which made me wonder if Adrienne Bellamy had called off the rest of the hits. I had told Director St. Clair all about her and my theory of her being the mastermind behind all the assassinations. But we had no tangible proof of anything yet. It was all circumstantial.

I needed to call Sterling in the Caymans. I wanted to call now, but more than likely, the phone was bugged. I opened it up to see; it was. I would have to wait until later. Sterling could probably give me some inside information on Adrienne, something I could use as leverage to get my family back.

After finishing my breakfast, I leaned back against the firm seat and let my thoughts consume me. My husband was my first thought. We had met at a retirement party for Director Ronald Keller. I had hated to see him go. He was smart and politically savvy, but he was also genuine. At least I thought so. Considering what had been going on in the bureau recently, I was starting to wonder about everybody. I remembered that I had been thirsty and had gone to get some punch from the fountain. Keyth was there already, filling his cup with the last of the punch.

When he became aware of my frustration, he offered me his cup and told me he could wait until the fountain was refilled. I smiled and told him I would wait with him. As we stood there, he told me that he worked in the Criminal Division, had grown up in Washington, and was a former D.C. police officer.

When they refilled the fountain, Keyth filled another cup, and we decided to take a walk outside. It was muggy, but neither of us complained. We must have walked for three hours around the building, which took up an entire block at E Street, between Ninth and Tenth Streets. Talking had been easy for both of us.

Looking back, I guess it was destiny that we met. I didn't know Keyth, and he had never heard of me. Just a chance meeting at a punch fountain launched a love affair that was still vibrant after eight years. I hated Coco Nimburu for what she was doing to us.

My life was as perfect as it could be before she came into it and literally wrecked it. I could feel my temper starting to flare, but there was nothing I could do. I would be on the train for another hour. Maybe I could find her on the train. She was no doubt wearing another flawless disguise, but I would know her by her eyes, I thought.

"Porter!" a man shouted after knocking.

I opened the door and let him in. It was the same man who had brought me the breakfast. He was a black man from Grenada with light brown eyes. I had checked him and the conductor out already.

"How many women are on the train?" I asked him.

"I do not know," he said, clearing my tray. "Would you like me to find out? It's no trouble."

"No," I told him, thinking she could be anyone on the train—even a man. She had even been me once. "I think I'll have a look around. I've never been anywhere first-class."

CHAPTER 74

M Y SEARCH was fruitless. I'm not by nature a pessimist, but I was
rapidly becoming one. Coco Nimburu was a highly intelligent,
professional assassin. I wasn't stupid either. I had graduated magna
cum laude, but I felt like an intellectual wimp right then. I was used to
being in charge, but now I was at someone else's mercy. Now I was
relegated to the corner with a dunce cap. Maybe I wasn't so smart after all.
What I had to do was minimize the mistakes. If I could do that, I could
come out of this thing in one piece—my family, too.

We pulled into Grand Central Station at 12:59 p.m. on the nose. The
cell rang. I knew it was my nemesis, but I wasn't anxious anymore. Before
I answered, I realized that I needed to call my master. It had been a very
long time since we had spoken. Ying Ming Lo used to say, "Everything has
its own time, Phoenix. You must learn to really relax." The interesting
thing was that I had learned to relax in battle, but in my personal life, I
wasn't quite where I knew I should be. Ying Ming Lo probably would tell
me that this thing with Coco Nimburu was designed to teach me something about myself. When this thing is over, I'm sure I will have learned
something worthwhile.

"It's your dime," I said impatiently.

"I trust you enjoyed the trip?" Coco said in Mandarin and waited for
an answer.

"To a point," I said, relaxing a little.

"Good, good. Did you enjoy your meal? You have to keep up your strength, you know."

"Am I supposed to think that you care about me now?" I bellowed.

"Actually, I do care. And when this thing is over, you'll know just how much. That, I promise."

"What do you want from me, Coco?"

"Tell me, Phoenix, do you understand the yin and yang?"

"What does that have to do with this? I really don't give a damn. I just want my family back."

Ignoring me, she went on to explain what she meant. "We are one and the same, Phoenix. You don't know it yet, but we are."

"You're a homicidal maniac. I'm an FBI agent, sworn to bring your ass to justice, which is what I'm going to do. One way or another."

"That's what I mean, Phoenix. Both of us have sworn an oath. Both of us have pledged our allegiance and offered our skills for principles we believe in. It is fitting that you end my life. It is fitting that my death propels you to a spiritual height you may not otherwise achieve. Do you really know yourself, my sister? Do you know that the fire that burns in you burns in me? Do you know that your desire to save life and my desire to take life comes from the same source?"

"If I want a philosophy lesson, I'll call Master Lo," I told her.

"Please do. He'll tell you the same thing." She laughed. "Enough chitchat. When you leave Grand Central Station, there will be a white stretch limousine waiting for you. The driver will take you to your next destination."

"I want to speak with my family," I demanded.

"I'll arrange it. Tell me this. Who said, 'You have offended my family. And you have offended a Shaolin Temple?' Ciao!"

The line disconnected. The quote was a line from *Enter the Dragon*. Actor and martial artist Bruce Lee had said it to his nemesis. What was Coco trying to tell me? I would figure it out later.

CHAPTER 75

THE LIMOUSINE stopped in front of the Intercontinental Hotel. My driver, whom I scrutinized to the point of aggravating him, opened my door. He told me to go to the register and a suite would be waiting for me. I think I was getting used to living the high life.

The lobby was filled with rich-looking people. The women were wearing elegant designer dresses and expensive jewelry. Their manicures probably had cost more than the silk Kung Fu uniform I was wearing. I felt so out of place.

I walked over to the front desk, wanting to get out of the lobby as soon as possible. "I'm Special Agent Phoenix Perry. You should have reservations for me."

The clerk looked me up and down, as if she didn't believe a word I was saying. It wasn't one of those racist looks I received from time to time. She was looking at me as if I didn't belong there, as if I were too low-class or something. I shook my head. The woman wasn't even a manager. She was just a lowly clerk wearing a cheap hotel blazer. Yet she was treating me as if she owned the place.

I reached for my credentials to show the bitch I could go anywhere I wanted. I could go behind that desk, throw her up against the wall, and frisk her in front of everybody, just to humiliate her the same way she was trying to humiliate me. Then I realized that I'd thrown everything, including my credentials, out of the train window. I looked at the clerk again. She curled her lips and shook her head.

"Look, Ho," I began. "I'm in a real bad mood! Just do your job and see if the registration is there."

The clerk laughed under her breath, which really irritated me. After hitting a few buttons on the computer terminal, she changed her attitude.

"I'm sorry, ma'am," the clerk said. "Adrienne Bellamy made the reservations. Everything's taken care of." She pulled out a computer card and a key. "The card is for the suite and this key is for the elevator. It will take you to the penthouse."

I rolled my eyes at her. What really angered me was that I was the same person she had disrespected not two minutes ago. Nothing about me had changed but suddenly I was getting the royal treatment. I felt like reporting her to the manager, but the truth was, I was just stressed by everything that was going on in my life.

"Where are the pay phones?" I asked her. If Adrienne Bellamy had paid for everything, the phone in my room was probably bugged. I needed to call Sterling Wise and find out what I could. I also needed to call the Manhattan field office to let them know where I was.

"The pay phones are over near the restrooms." She frowned and pointed her finger over my shoulder.

She was probably wondering why I didn't go to my suite and call from there. But I wasn't going to explain myself to this heifer. "Do you have a Susan Lucci or a Debbie Morgan registered here?"

She hit a few buttons on the keyboard. "No, I'm sorry, we don't."

"What's the cost of my room?" I asked, curious to know how much rich people paid for what amounted to a bed and breakfast.

"Fifteen-hundred dollars a night."

The surprise on my face must have been obvious because she laughed. I could see why she had such a pompous attitude. She must have thought I was one of New York's many vagrants who had wandered in looking for a handout.

I went to the pay phone, studying everyone around me. Coco Nimburu could be any one of them. She was in the hotel. I knew it. It was how she operated. I would be getting a call from her. I was sure of it.

My first call on the pay phone was to the bureau's Manhattan office. I let them know where I was and told them to give me plenty of room. They promised to send me a package with my credentials and a communications device by special messenger. Then I had them connect me to the Renegade Hotel and Casino in the Caymans. Before long, Sterling was on the phone.

"Attorney Wise," he said.

"Sterling. It's Agent Perry. I need to speak with you. I know Adrienne Bellamy was your client. I'm not asking for any privileged attorney-client information. I just need to know what to expect. She has my husband and daughter."

"I'm sorry to hear that, Agent Perry. I don't know if I can help or not. But what you should expect is a bribe of some sort. She flaunts her wealth and offers you whatever it is she thinks you want. It's very seductive, but don't give into it. If you do, it will only come back to haunt you later. Tell me, what have you found out so far?"

"I know she's black pretending to be white."

"Then you have the upper hand. With that information, she'll tell you everything else. But be careful. She's dangerous as hell, even though she doesn't appear to be. What she reveals will be the truth, but she will use it against you later. She can't afford to have people know who she really is. I can't stress that point enough. A lot of people have died because they knew what you now know. Be careful."

"I will," I said.

CHAPTER 76

THE PENTHOUSE was extravagant, to say the least. Opulence was woven into the décor with its marble pillars and floor. The three-bedroom suite had every imaginable amenity: a stocked bar and refrigerator, a bathrobe and slippers, a fax machine, a large-screen TV with VCR and DVD, and a state-of-the-art stereo system that Keyth would kill for. Expensive Persian rugs were strategically placed throughout the sumptuous penthouse. It even had a kitchen with china and silverware. The lavish suite was seductive, just as Sterling had warned me.

In the dining room, a floor-to-ceiling picture window provided a breathtaking view. I went out on the terrace and looked down at Central Park, which looked like an endless forest. Manhattan was beautiful from up here. I felt hungry again and decided to order room service.

Picking up the menu, I looked at the prices. They were ridiculous, but what the hell. I wasn't paying for it. The lobster from Maine looked good, so I ordered it. The telephone in my suite rang, and I knew it was Coco. When I reached the telephone, I saw the message light flashing.

"Hello, Coco," I said.

"Agent Perry, this is Adrienne Bellamy. I'm en route from Morocco. I trust everything in the suite is to your liking?"

"Everything is fine," I told her, a little surprised that she had called. "I'm concerned about my husband and daughter. I haven't heard from them."

"Have you checked your messages?"

"No. I wasn't aware that I had messages until a moment ago."

"Well, listen to them. I'm sure they'll put you at ease," she said, her voice full of confidence. "Now, you and I have something to discuss. There are some things you need to understand. Before you jump to conclusions, hear my side of the story; then decide what to do."

"Director St. Clair already knows who you are and what you did," I told her. "There's no point in continuing this vendetta."

"Just hear me out; that's all I ask," she said convincingly. "Let me handle Director St. Clair. I think what I have to say will be of great interest to you. You don't have the whole picture. I can fill in some gaps for you. When you've seen the complete picture, then you'll be in a position to judge. Think about it. That's all I ask."

"Okay," I said. "But I really don't see how anything you have to say could justify killing FBI agents, your sister, NSA Director Pockets, my father, and so many others. Is being black that terrible?"

"Be patient. I'll explain everything tonight."

CHAPTER 77

ADRIENNE BELLAMY told me to be patient, as if I had any other choice. She was holding all the cards. I was just waiting for her to deal. I pushed the message button on the phone and heard Savannah's voice.

"Hi, Mommy! Guess where we are? We're in Disney World! It's hot down here, too. But me and Daddy are having so much fun. Daddy said we can come home soon. We won't be in any more danger. Well, see you soon, Mommy!"

I was hoping a message from Keyth was next, but there was nothing from him. He's just having the time of his life, I thought. He was probably having sex with Coco every hour. My anger was starting to simmer again. I took a deep breath and let it out slowly, wondering if our marriage could survive this.

I loved Keyth, but the images of him and Coco kept invading my mind. I'm nice-looking, but I'm very small. Never had a voluptuous body or anything like that, been thin all my life. After having Savannah, I lost the weight quickly, in the breasts, too. Now that Keyth has had the needles and Coco, I didn't know how to compete with that.

CHAPTER 78

"ROOM SERVICE!" I heard the waiter say after knocking. At least the food was there. That would make me feel better. After eating, I watched television for a couple of hours. I still hadn't heard from Coco. I decided to go down to Central Park and walk off the food I'd just devoured. Walking through the park, I thought about what Coco had quoted from the film *Enter the Dragon*. "You have offended my family. And you have offended a Shaolin Temple," Bruce Lee had said in the film. Coco had also mentioned that she and I were the same. Somehow, yin and yang played a role in her philosophical sophistry.

I sat down on a park bench and watched the endless parade of tourists snapping pictures and pointing at historical sites. About ten feet away from me, a woman and a child were playing with a Frisbee. A moment or two later, the yellow toy floated to me, and I caught it. A little girl with blonde hair ran over to retrieve her toy. I smiled, thinking of my own daughter, who wasn't aware that she was being held against her will. The little blonde girl smiled at me bashfully. Children are so precious when they're that young, I thought. What happens to them to turn them into the Coco Nimburus and Adrienne Bellamys of the world?

"Hi!" She smiled. "May I have my Frisbee, please?"

Her manner of speaking led me to believe she was from a well-to-do family who were probably sending her to one of the excellent private schools in the Manhattan area.

"Sure, honey," I said, handing it to her.

"That's a Kung Fu uniform," she said with wonder in her innocent bright blue eyes.

"Yes, it is," I told her. "How did you know?"

"Cartoons."

I saw her mother coming to get her child. She was blonde also and reminded me of former WWF wrestler, Sable. Two tough-looking men, who may have been bodyguards, accompanied her. I wondered why she needed bodyguards.

"You look sad," the child said to me.

"Sharon," her mother called out, "Don't bother her, honey. Come on back over here."

"She's no bother," I said. "She's adorable."

"Thank you. That's kind of you to say," the mother said and gasped. Her eyes looked vacant and then she fell forward. A shuriken was stuck in the back of her head. The suddenness of her death was shocking. Coco had struck again and had already vanished.

CHAPTER 79

T HE VICTIM was Chase Davenport, Sterling Wise's girlfriend. Agent
Cooper, one of her bodyguards, told me that she had insisted on
coming to the park. She had complained endlessly about getting out
of her apartment. He was overwhelmed with guilt. A woman he was
charged with protecting had been killed right in front of her daughter.
Seeing her mother killed would probably haunt the little girl the rest of
her life.

After four hours with New York's finest, I had one of the bureau techs
patch the call with the Renegade Hotel and Casino in the Caymans so I
could inform Sterling of Chase Davenport's murder. He told me that they
had met at Georgetown Law School fifteen years ago. They had carried
on a lustful affair while she was engaged to marry the son of one of
Manhattan's leading families.

The relationship continued after Chase married and had lasted longer
than most marriages. Sterling was deeply distressed when I told him about
her death. He had lost two friends because of Adrienne Bellamy. Whatever
her secret was, it couldn't have been worth all this. Nothing was that
important.

I was drained and needed to lie down. The senseless killing of a defense-
less mother in front of her daughter had siphoned off what little strength
I had left. As I approached the elevator, the arrogant clerk who had
checked me in handed me a briefcase she had received from a courier.

"No one can go up to the penthouse without being announced. Even if it's the FBI," she said in her haughty tone.

An assortment of invectives came to mind, but I didn't use any of them. I thanked her and went up to the penthouse. On the way up, I opened the briefcase and saw the electronic communications equipment, which consisted of a phone and an earpiece that operated as a microphone and a hearing device. The elevator doors opened, and I walked into my high-rise dwelling for the night.

The message on the telephone light was flashing. I hoped it was my husband or daughter, but the way things were going, I was sure it would be more bad news. I almost didn't push the button, but I did. Coco Nimburu had left me another message.

"What's the matter, Phoenix?" Coco said, speaking English for the first time. I assumed there was no reason to hide who she was and what she was doing. "You looked so sad on that park bench, like you had the weight of the world on your shoulders." She laughed, and it infuriated me. However, she became serious, saying, "I could have killed you all. I wouldn't have killed Davenport if you had agreed to grant my request. Her death is on your head, not mine. I was perfectly content with stopping the killings, but, again, you needed incentive. Who's next? You never know who I'm going to get next, but you know I will go on killing and killing until someone worthy kills me. You can put an end to all of it tonight. Or I can go on killing for a price, and indiscriminately. Get some rest! You're going to need it!"

Still conflicted about killing her, I went to the bedroom and fell face forward on the bed. Having been stripped of all sense of pride as a federal agent, I wept. I wept for myself and for the little girl whom I had just met. Then it occurred to me what Coco was trying to tell me.

When our morality is tested to its limit, we adjust our morality to justify our actions. Bruce Lee had to kill his nemesis in the movie, not simply because he wanted to, but because it was necessary. His archenemy would have gone on killing and peddling dope, becoming more and more corrupt, devastating countless families. I was going to have to kill Coco Nimburu. It was the only way to stop the carnage.

CHAPTER 80

I WAS AWAKENED by the loud ringing of my telephone. I looked at the clock. It was 10 P.M. Saliva had found its way out of my mouth and onto the pillow. I was in a fog, my mind still coming out of the deep slumber. In a raspy voice, I mumbled, "Hello."

"Be downstairs in ten minutes," Coco commanded. "Your driver is waiting for you." Then she hung up.

I picked up the cell phone issued to me by the FBI. I pushed the power button several times, but it wouldn't come on. I opened the back of the phone to check the batteries. There weren't any. That meant that Coco, probably wearing her Phoenix Perry disguise had intercepted it while I was out in the park. Then she changed disguises and gave the briefcase to the clerk. I shook my head in disgust and anger. Coco was right about one thing. Tonight, it would be all over. I was going to end it.

I put her communication device in my ear, sure that she would be on the air soon to give me further instructions and probably gloat. On the way to the lobby, I thought about what had happened in Central Park. I remembered the little girl, and my anger flared up. I was a walking inferno, ready to unleash the fire that burned within. I walked through the lobby so focused and concentrated on what I had to do that it seemed as if I were moving in slow motion.

When I came out of the lobby onto Central Park West, I was awakened by the sounds of the city that never sleeps. My driver opened the door of the stretch limousine for me, and I got in. A few minutes later, we were headed toward the seedy side of Manhattan that most people outside New York don't see or hear about.

"Right on time," I heard Coco say in the earpiece. She laughed. "I would love to have seen your face when you realized you'd been duped again. Don't worry; I let the agent who delivered the electronics live. This is so much fun. Too bad we have to die, huh, Phoenix?"

"Oh, you're going to die all right," I said. "It's just a matter of time now."

"Do I detect a note of hostility?" Coco asked, still snickering in my ear. Hearing her constantly laughing at me made me even more homicidal. "I see you've figured out what I was trying to tell you, my sister. Tell me. Now that you understand, are we so different?"

I didn't answer. The question was strangely disturbing, penetrating every stratum of my personal ethics and morality. I convinced myself that killing Coco Nimburu was better than the alternative; it was better than her killing my family or me. It was better than her killing Kelly, Sterling Wise, or Victoria Warren. Killing Coco Nimburu was good. It was good for society. It was good for the judicial system. Her death would save the system millions of dollars in trial costs, prison, and the endless appeals. Yes, killing her would be good for everyone—especially me.

"Your silence says it all, Phoenix," Coco continued. "Promise me something."

"What's that, Coco?" I asked, wondering what new chore I had to complete.

"Promise me you will be merciless. I want to go out in a battle. I want my life to end as I have lived it. No regrets and no second thoughts about anything I've done in the flesh. My fate was sealed the moment I was conceived. All that I have done was leading up to this moment—and I welcome it. So, will you? Will you be merciless?"

"What about my family? If I do what you want, will they be released?"

"I am an honest woman. This I promise you. They will be released and will be free from harm."

"Then I will do as you ask."

CHAPTER 81

THE LIMOUSINE STOPPED in front of a bedraggled bar called The Spot. The driver opened my door, and I got out.

"I think it's time we met," I heard Coco say after a long silence. She had been conspicuously quiet for about fifteen minutes, which was usual for her. I was getting used to her philosophizing and endless nefarious banter. "Come on in. I'm waiting for you."

The air was foul in this ill-kept part of Manhattan. A bum, wearing clothes that probably hadn't been washed in a year, was urinating against a wall covered with graffiti. Two prostitutes wearing little more than a thong were sharing a crack pipe. Empty malt liquor bottles were everywhere. Burger King wrappers were at my feet.

This is a strange place for a battle, I thought. Nevertheless, I would do what I had to do here or wherever Coco chose to die.

The people on the street stared at me as if I were a rock star slumming and looking for quick thrills. I could hear the thunderous bass of the loud music being played inside the bar. The tune sounded familiar, but I couldn't remember the name of it. I walked in and heard the voice of Leroy "Sugarfoot" Bonner of the Ohio Players singing "Skin Tight."

I saw a woman standing in the midst of a crowded bar full of black men and women and a few Puerto Ricans. She was holding a mug of beer and raised it as if she were toasting me. Was this a joke to her, I thought? We were about to engage in mortal combat, and she was having a beer in a loud bar like nothing was going on? She had a lot of nerve. My family was at her mercy, and here she was, playing with me as if I were her personal toy. I could see Coco's lips moving and heard her voice in my ear.

"Come on over and have a beer."

Finally, I had come face to face with Coco Nimburu. I don't know what I had expected, but I certainly didn't expect to see such a beautiful woman with such a tight body. I could tell she worked out regularly. She was Japanese with long, flowing black hair.

I was just about to go over there and knock that smile off her face when I was punched in the jaw. The blow sent me spiraling out of control against the oak bar. Everything seemed to be moving in slow motion—except for Coco's laughter in my ear. My jaw had been broken, and the pain was agonizing. Ying Ming Lo had warned me of this very thing many times. My anger had gotten me flattened by an unexpected punch.

If I had been in control of my anger, I would have been able to feel the antagonism in the air. I would have been able to intercept the blow or to redirect it away from me. In either case, my jaw wouldn't have been broken. But the blow was sobering in that it awakened me spiritually.

"You got a lotta goddamn nerve coming in here after what you did," my assailant yelled.

Then I heard Coco say, "Oh, I forgot to tell you—you came in here earlier and robbed these people at gunpoint. I think they're a little pissed." She laughed again. "I told you—you have a lot to prove. If you can get out of here in one piece, I'll know I've got the right woman for the job."

Having a broken jaw helped me put my anger aside so that I could focus on what was happening. An angry crowd was gathering, hurling insults at me, racial invectives included, in their array of embittered words.

"We gon' kill you, bitch," I heard someone yell.

"I'm gonna cut you every way but loose," I heard another man say.

He pulled a switchblade, and the sharp blade snapped out. It was life or death with these people, and I wasn't about to take it easy on them. The man with the switchblade was the immediate threat. I had to take him out first. He made a move toward me with the blade, and I kicked it out of his hand with a front snap kick. The blade flew up in the air and stuck into the ceiling. Then I kicked him in the head with a reverse hook kick, knocking him out cold.

My skill as a martial artist didn't scare anyone. They were all still determined to attack me. I sensed a blow coming from the right. It was the same guy who had broken my jaw. I redirected his blow, but the bar patrons were all coming at the same time. I feinted at the nearest man, which caused him to hesitate long enough for me to kick the next man. While my foot was still in the air, I whipped it in the direction of the man who had broken my jaw, connecting with flesh and bone. Both men were unconscious.

The man who had hesitated now ran toward me at full speed. I bent my knees just before he reached me and used his weight and speed against him. As I stood up, I threw him over the bar and into the mirror. I heard the sound of glass breaking behind me. The bar patrons were still coming at me.

I stepped into the midst of them. One was coming to my right, another to my left. The man to my right was about to swing, but I was ahead of him. I hit him with a left right left combination. He was out before he knew what had hit him. I was blocking and striking everyone near me. People were falling all around me, and still they came.

A bottle of beer sailed across the room. I ducked just in time, and it hit the bartender in the face. Another bottle flew toward me while I was in the middle of a palm strike. I caught the bottle and hit the woman to my left in the head with it. Using the same bottle, I hit several attackers, then threw it back across the room and hit the man who had thrown it in the face.

I sensed immediate danger behind me, but before I could turn to face my assailant, a shuriken whistled past my head. Then another whistled by. Coco was a deadly assassin. If she were trying to hit me, she would have.

A woman groaned behind me. I turned around to see what had happened. The woman had pulled a gun from her purse and was obviously preparing to shoot me. One shuriken was stuck in her throat and another in her forehead, right between the eyes. Blood was sliding down her face and mixed with the blood coming out of her throat.

Distracted by the death of the woman behind me, I felt someone grab me by my uniform. I grabbed his hand and twisted his wrist.

"You're breaking my fuckin' arm!" he shouted.

I held on to him and continued the battle. Using my legs, I was able to kick a few more of my attackers. Several ran for their lives. Applying more pressure to his wrist, I forced him to bend over. I kicked him in the face a couple of times. As I let him fall to the ground, another man grabbed my arm. I swung the arm he had grabbed in a circular motion, raising it above his head. I punched him in the stomach, then lifted him off his feet and threw him into the shattered mirror.

Looking around, I saw that my attackers were stretched out on the floor, and the bar was empty. Coco must have left with the other fleeing patrons. When I walked out of the bar, the driver was waiting for me with the limousine door open. I got in, and we headed toward the financial district.

CHAPTER 82

T HE TWIN TOWERS of the World Trade Center were my next stop. The limousine driver again opened my door, and I got out. The vibration from walking on the cement caused my jaw to ache more than before. It needed to be wired so it could heal properly. The driver opened the glass door to One World Trade Center for me. I remembered that Adrienne Bellamy had an office here. I assumed I was about to meet the queen bee herself.

"Saving your life is becoming a full-time job, Phoenix," I heard Coco say in my ear. "Ever see the film *Interview with the Vampire*?"

"Yes," I said through clenched teeth.

"I'm feeling a little like Tom Cruise, trying to get the killer in you to come forth," she laughed. "Make no mistake, Phoenix; you are a killer!" She laughed again, borrowing a line from the film. "Take the elevator to the 102nd floor. They're waiting for you."

"They?" I questioned, hoping she would tell me whom I was meeting other than Adrienne Bellamy.

"Ebony and Ivory, together in perfect harmony," she joked, singing the Stevie Wonder and Paul McCartney hit.

She was telling me that Winston Keyes would be there also. "Where are you going to be?" I asked, stepping into the elevator.

"Around."

The elevator door opened a couple of minutes later, and I saw Winston

Keyes standing in front of an office door. He was well-groomed, sporting a trimmed moustache and wearing a black suit with thin pinstripes.

"This way, Agent Perry," he said, politely. "That's a nasty bruise you've got there."

I didn't say anything. Talking brought more pain, and I wasn't a masochist. At this point, I was more interested in finding out why Adrienne Bellamy had done all of this. What could her reason possibly be? What explanation was she going to give me that would justify all of this?

I walked into the outer office expecting to see her, but I would have to wait a bit longer. I saw another set of doors that probably led to her inner sanctum. Winston Keyes opened both doors as if I were about to meet the Queen of Egypt.

I found myself almost peering around the doors as he opened them, curious to see the woman who had ordered the deaths of so many people. She was sitting at her desk with the phone to her ear. When she saw me, she motioned me to come in and pointed at one of two leather chairs in front of her large circular desk. It was hard to believe that this blue-eyed blonde was a black woman. She was tan and looked to be about fifty-five years old.

The large diamond earring on her desk had my attention now. Adrienne Bellamy had taken it off so she could use the phone. It must have cost a small fortune. I wondered how many karats the earrings were. Were they Cartier diamonds? Then I saw the diamond on her finger, which was much larger than those in the earrings.

As I patiently waited for her to conclude her conversation, I admired her taste in clothing. She was wearing what I thought was a red Louis Vuitton suit. The collar and buttons were black, which matched her black cashmere blouse. I resisted the urge to look under the desk to see what kind of shoes she was wearing.

She finally hung up. "My work is never done," Adrienne Bellamy said. "I'm trying to build a casino in Sun City, South Africa, near the spectacular Palace of the Lost City Hotel. We're scheduled to break ground a month from now." She looked at the bruise on my slightly swollen jaw. "Are you okay?"

I nodded.

"I suppose you're waiting for an explanation, right?" she asked.

I nodded again.

She reached across the desk and turned around a picture of a handsome white man who looked just like her. "Do you know who this is?" she asked.

I shook my head, trying to avoid as much pain as I could.

"This is Sean Bellamy, my son and your next president. He'll be running as an independent in the next election."

I closed my eyes. It was clear now. She was wiping out everybody who knew he was black. "What does Victoria Warren have to do with this?" I forced myself to say through clenched teeth.

"Ms. Warren was a former girlfriend I paid off to have an abortion. I had told Sean to break it off with her. I have always had big plans for him. I wasn't about to let a little thing like love stand in the way of acquiring 1600 Pennsylvania Avenue."

"I see; and Sterling Wise handled the Warren family for you?"

She nodded. "He didn't tell you any of this? I'm surprised. When Coco made the attempt on his life, I thought he'd spill his guts. A huge mistake on my part. Had I known he would keep his mouth shut, I never would have targeted him."

"So Cynthia Charles and Chase Davenport were killed for nothing?" I asked in amazement.

"Apparently so," she said in a ho-hum tone. "People say a lot of things to their lovers. I tell Winston everything in bed. It is our most intimate time together. I assumed that most people told their lovers their secrets. I was wrong in Sterling's case."

I shook my head in disgust. "Do you realize a woman was killed today in front of her child because of your family skeletons?"

"Coco did that on her own. I told her to stop the killings. I wanted to speak with you to see if we could come to some sort of accommodation."

I didn't mean to, but I laughed in her face, which hurt like hell. The woman had killed repeatedly and thought that an accommodation could be reached with the FBI? This was insanity.

"You don't kill people for the presidency," I told her.

"Really," she said, skeptically. "You still believe that after what you've learned so far? You already have corruption at the highest levels of government. Look at the list of people who've been killed. Clayton Pockets was killed because he was trying to blackmail me. That degenerate gambler was so deep in debt that he was on the verge of selling government secrets to China. If I hadn't stepped in, who knows what the enemies of this country would have acquired from the NSA Director.

"Director Pockets had gotten the information from Gordon Scott, the NSA communications tech. He was doing a favor for your father, who sold the information to Jericho, Sterling Wise's older brother, a notorious drug and munitions dealer in the Cayman Islands. When I learned who leaked the information to Jericho, I offered your father a business opportunity to keep this information quiet. The business you own thrives because of my generosity."

"None of the people you killed did anything to deserve death," I said with righteous indignation. "And even if they had, who gave you the right to judge?"

"Haven't you judged Coco Nimburu?" she asked. "Is she worthy of death?"

"What about your sister and Senator Blevins?" I asked, avoiding the question.

"I'll just say this, Agent Perry. My being black and pretending to be white was expedient—a means to an end. I was very beautiful in my youth, and men of all races wanted me. I was one of a few women who realized that sex was the great equalizer in a male-dominated society. My father was white, but society said I was black. I have no problem with being black, but looking white offered far more advantages. I could go places that most blacks couldn't. It was easy to blend in with whites in college."

"Is that where you met Senator Blevins? In college?" I asked through clenched teeth.

"Yes. Martha Blevins and I were like two peas in a pod. We shared everything, exchanged clothes, and drank out of the same glass. Martha introduced me to Jason in college. I didn't know I was going to fall in love with her brother. When Jason told her he wanted to marry me, she was genuinely happy for us. But I hadn't told Jason I was black. I toyed with the idea of never telling him. He would never know the difference. I didn't mean to deceive him. My race just wasn't an issue until he asked me to marry him.

"I agonized over the decision and decided that if he had a problem with my being black, he wasn't the man of my dreams. When I told him, he was shocked, but his feelings hadn't changed. He told me we could never tell anyone the truth. I agreed. He trusted Martha, and so did I. So we told her together. The look of disgust on her face said it all. She no longer wanted to have anything to do with me. Jason was as shocked by her reaction as I was. They argued and didn't speak to each other for months.

"Jason and I eloped, fearing that Martha would eventually tell their parents. She never did, but she did everything in her power to make my life miserable. On holidays and at family dinners, she would tell black jokes at the table, knowing I would have to go along or reveal the truth. The jokes wounded me deeply. It felt as if someone had stuck a dagger in my heart and twisted it. I pretended the jokes were funny like everyone else, but I was dying inside."

"What about Judge Taylor? Why would you have your own sister killed?"

"She wouldn't listen to reason. Jennifer's been stubborn all of her life. I asked her to keep quiet about being Sean's aunt. She refused and threatened to go public the moment he announced his intention to run for the presidency. She could never see the big picture, haranguing me about the evils of slavery and how Sean could be living proof that the one-drop rule was just as absurd today as it was when the colonies adopted it four hundred years ago.

"Jennifer really believed Sean's true ancestry wouldn't stand in the way of gaining the highest office in the land. I know better. If people knew he was black, it would ruin his chances of winning the Oval Office. People would come up with carefully constructed arguments to persuade the American public not to take him seriously as a presidential candidate. They would ask questions like, 'How can we trust a man who has hidden who he is all of his life?' Or they'd say, 'If he's ashamed of who he is, how can he represent the country honorably?' You know I'm right, Phoenix.

"Believe me, I'm not the first person to kill in order to gain political power. What do you think the CIA is all about? The average American sticks his head in the proverbial sand when it comes to what we do to other countries. Then they wonder why we have so many enemies. Do you really think the Iranians would have dared take hostages if we hadn't backed the Shah? Do you think any president's hands are clean? We're constantly overthrowing governments and setting up dictators we can control. If that means killing people to achieve that end, we do it. It's that simple."

I had to admit she was making a lot of sense, but I wasn't persuaded in the slightest. She was going to jail, but I needed to know if Sean had been in on her murderous campaign. If he wasn't, I saw no reason to drag him into it.

"Does your son know you're committing murder to further his political ambitions?" I asked.

"No. Sean is completely in the dark," she said. "I'm his mother. I have to look out for his best interests."

I heard a shuriken whistle through the air and then a sudden gasp behind me. I turned around and saw the surprised look on Winston's face before he fell dead to the carpeted floor. He'd had a silenced gun pointed at the back of my head. Adrienne reached into her desk and pulled out a revolver, but it was too late. Another shuriken whistled past my ear and sank deeply into her head. Coco Nimburu ran out of the office and I chased her.

CHAPTER 83

A S I BOLTED through the outer office door, I saw Coco running down the hallway. She took the exit stairs. I was right behind her. I could hear her laughing as we ran up several flights of stairs.

"Having fun yet, Phoenix?" Coco's voice echoed in the stairwell.

Severe pain shot through my jaw as I ran up flight after flight. I finally made it to the roof. Apparently, she wanted the battle to take place there. Opening the door cautiously, I saw Coco Nimburu waiting for me. I stepped onto the roof and caught my breath.

"You know they were going to kill you, don't you?" Coco asked calmly. She was wearing a black ninja uniform. "You owe me your life."

"You sure you wanna do this?" I asked her. Strangely, the pain in my jaw seemed to have lessened. I sharpened my focus and was ready for anything.

"I didn't spare your life for nothing," Coco said grimly. Her sense of humor was gone. "Weapons?" She opened a black case with red velvet interior, which contained swords, shuriken, and other weapons in it.

I shook my head and walked to within five feet of her. "Is there anything else I should know?" I asked.

"Your family's at home and safe," Coco assured me. "You'll be getting a package soon."

"A package?" I asked, as we bowed to each other. As we circled each other, we talked to each other like old school chums, yet we were about to engage in hand-to-hand combat to the death. Unlike in the movies, a martial art challenge does not take long. A real life duel never does.

"You'll understand when you get it," Coco said. "Use your best judgment, my sister."

With lightning speed, Coco kicked at my head. I was light on my feet, which enabled me to avoid the powerful blow. Moving forward, I began with a token lead kick designed to distract her. It was quick and powerful, but token nevertheless. She blocked it with ease just as I knew she would, but left herself open for a perfectly timed reverse hook kick to the head. The blow dazed her long enough for me to follow up with three rapid roundhouse kicks to her head. Coco fell to the ground and shook the cobwebs away.

"I can't believe I fell for that weak kick," Coco said and stood to her feet. Before I knew it, she was on the offensive, throwing kicks and strikes from every direction. I blocked them all, but she was able to set me up with a token strike, too. She back-fisted me, then spun around and kicked me in the head. I fell to the ground.

I got up quickly and riposted. Coco was a master martial artist, too. With the exception of being blindsided in the bar I had just left, no one had knocked me down since I had left the tutelage of Ying Ming Lo—at least when I was ready. The guy in the bar had gotten lucky. Back on my toes, I was moving with purpose again, determined to whittle down her defense first, and then destroy her.

Suddenly, I sensed a hostile presence other than Coco on the roof, and I thought I knew who it was. What was he waiting for? I wondered. Why was he lurking in the shadows?

We engaged in a series of attacks. After each series, I kicked Coco in the leg. Nothing powerful but enough to hurt and distract. We engaged again, and I briefly looked at the leg I had kicked before initiating my attack. She thought I was going to kick her there again. Instead, I feinted with my left leg. When she attempted to block it, she was wide open. I kicked her hard with the right. She was hurt, and I moved in, throwing a left-right-left combination and finishing with a powerful kick to the head that put Coco on her ass again.

Coco stood to her feet, but staggered a little. Still dazed, she grabbed a sword from the black case and came after me with it. She wasn't ready to die after all, I thought. I did several reverse somersaults to get away from her. She came after me, swinging the sharp blade. I was near the edge of the roof with nowhere to go but down. Coco pointed the sword at me and said, "I guess you weren't good enough after all. Tell God I said hello and I'll see him later."

She drew the sword back to swing it like a baseball bat. The sight of someone swinging a sword at them would have paralyzed most people. But I knew it was my only chance to escape. Just before she brought the blade forward, I quickly moved forward and kicked her in the head. Then I somersaulted over to the weapons case.

I grabbed a sword to defend myself. I wanted to grab a shuriken or two to throw at the presence I felt once I dispensed with Coco, but I didn't have time. She was coming after me again. We engaged in a series of thrusts and parries. The sound of the blades colliding was loud—sparks flew. I stayed on the offensive, looking for the one opening that would give me an opportunity to end the battle.

We engaged again. This time I kicked her in the right leg again. Each time I kicked her, she grew angrier. Just as my anger had dulled my senses and led to a broken jaw, her anger would hasten her death. I was sure Coco was not aware of the presence on the roof. Otherwise, she would have tried to kill the intruder, I thought.

My constant kicks to her leg reduced her mobility. She was limping a little, but still dangerous. We engaged again, and I feinted at the now-injured leg. She protected the leg, leaving her self open again, and I kicked her in the head. She went down. This time she was slow getting up.

Somehow, she found the strength and attacked furiously, but I was in control now. Coco Nimburu was mine. Patiently, I blocked each attack effortlessly. When I felt she was at the end of her attack, I blocked the strike and hit her in the head with the handle of my sword. The blow dazed her, and with one clean slice I took her head before she had a chance to riposte.

I had been merciless, just like she wanted me to be. For a second or two, she just stood there looking at me—vacant eyed—frozen in time. Then her head fell off her shoulders. Her lifeless body clasped. The nightmare was over. The great Coco Nimburu was dead.

CHAPTER 84

BLOOD WAS EVERYWHERE. I looked down at the body of the woman who had murdered my father and my students and felt remorse—even though I knew killing Coco Nimburu was the only way to stop her murderous rampage. I thought her death would bring me some measure of satisfaction, but it didn't. I could feel the intruder's presence even more strongly now that Coco was dead.

As I walked over to the weapons case, I kept wondering what the intruder was waiting for. I stooped and looked into the case. The silver shuriken sparkled in the moonlight. I picked up one of the perfectly balanced weapons and realized it had been used to save my life several times that very night. I slipped one in my jacket pocket.

It had occurred to me that someone other than Michelson was on Adrienne Bellamy's payroll. How else had Coco Nimburu known where the safe house was? Michelson had been murdered before I had told Agent James to move my family. Michelson couldn't have told her where the new safe house was.

That would explain why the FBI hadn't arrived. They had to know something was wrong when they couldn't contact me. And wouldn't they have followed me here? Just then, I saw the intruder who had watched my battle with Coco Nimburu. The nightmare wasn't over after all. I eased the shuriken out of my pocket and readied myself to throw it if necessary. The figure stepped out of the shadows, and pointed a gun at me.

"I was hoping it wouldn't come to this, Agent Perry," St. Clair said.

I was staring down the barrel of a Smith & Wesson .38-caliber pistol.

"Why, sir? Why would you throw away your career?"

"I can think of ten million reasons. I was almost there. I was so close," he babbled.

"Money?" I heard myself say. "Is that what this is about?"

"It's always about money, Phoenix. You know that."

"Director St. Clair, are you sure you want to do this?"

"I have to, Phoenix. I'm too old to go to prison, and I'm not ready to die. I'm sorry. I always liked you."

I could sense that he was about to shoot. I dived and rolled on the ground just before he squeezed off a couple of rounds. The bullets whistled past me. I threw the shuriken from a kneeling position when I regained my balance. The eight-sided blade ripped into his forehead, and St. Clair died instantly.

My mind was made up. I was going to keep as much of this out of the papers as I could. I had killed Coco Nimburu. I was going to make the most of her death. I would blame it all on her. There would be no explanation for the murders. No one had to know what had really happened. Adrienne Bellamy and Winston Keyes would become two more victims on her list of casualties. With Coco, Michelson, and St. Clair dead, who could contradict me? No one knew about Coco's letters except me and Kelly, and I knew she could be trusted with that secret. Yes. Coco Nimburu would become another John Wilkes Booth or James Earl Ray. If Sean Bellamy decided to run for the presidency, I wasn't going to be the one to ruin his chances. After all, he had had nothing to do with any of this.

EPILOGUE
CHAPTER 85

THE LIMOUSINE DRIVER had been paid handsomely to take me wherever I needed to go. After I had explained everything to the Manhattan field office and NYPD, the driver drove me to the hospital to get my jaw wired. When that was completed, I was driven back to Washington. I walked into my house at 9:30 A.M.

When I opened the door, my daughter ran across the room and leaped into my arms. "Mommy!" she cried out. "I missed you, Mommy!"

"I missed you too, precious," I said through clenched teeth.

My bundle of joy pulled back and looked at my bruised jaw. "What happened to your face?"

"I wasn't ready, and a man hit me."

"That's not fair," she said, consoling me. "Did ya get 'em, Mommy? Did ya give it to 'em good?"

I nodded.

"How many was it?" I heard my husband ask me. He was standing in the doorway of the dining room. I stood up and looked at him. Images of him and Coco flooded my mind.

"A lot. Maybe twenty or so."

The doorbell rang, and I opened the door.

"Package for Phoenix Perry," the Federal Express driver said.

"That's you, Mommy," my daughter reminded me.

"Sign here," the woman said. "There's another box in my van. I'll get it."

After I signed, she gave me a long tubular package. While I waited for the driver to return, I opened it. Inside was an ivory-handled sword with yin and yang symbols on it. I slid the blade out of its sheath and read the words on it, which were written in Mandarin. Coco Nimburu's name was engraved on one side and my name on the other. It was her way of telling me that we were two sides of the same coin.

The sword was beautiful and, in spite of myself, I was touched by the gesture. There was also a letter inside the tube. I opened it.

Dear Phoenix,

Thanks to you, I was able to leave this world on my own terms. As a token of my appreciation, I'm leaving you my sword and my personal journals. The journals may be worth something in the literary world. Read them and do what you think is best. As for my remains, cremate me and empty my ashes on the Paramount Studios lot. I think I would have made a great actress. What do you think?

You're probably wondering why I chose you to handle the arrangements. I want you to remember me. Remember that I wasn't all bad. There was some good in me. As long as you're alive and remember me, I will live, too. Enjoy life, Phoenix. You only have one. Live it to the fullest.

Your sister in life and in death,
Coco Nimburu

P.S. I didn't have sex with Keyth. I just needed you to think I did. You know, incentive. HA-HA-HA! It worked, didn't it? I left you enough money to take a leave of absence and open a new dojo. But do with it what you will.

CHAPTER 86

AFTER READING THE LETTER, I ran to my husband and threw my arms around him. Tears ran down my cheeks. I had had many teachers in my life, but none of them had taught me more about myself than the Assassin who had terrorized the D.C. area this past June. Ying Ming Lo had told me a willing student could learn from anyone. Pushed to the limit, I was a killer, too.

I was due for an extended vacation, so Keyth and I decided to take Savannah to San Francisco. We took her to all the sights in that international city. We ate lunch at Mister Big Stuff's World Famous Barbecue every day. As I looked out at the bay, I could see Alcatraz, and I thought of the woman whom I had killed without mercy, just as she had asked. In a strange way, I missed her laugh and the games she had played with me. I still didn't know if I was ready to leave the bureau, but I had been giving it a lot of thought.

After spending a week in San Francisco, we flew down to the City of Angels. I was going to do as Coco Nimburu had asked and deliver her remains to the Paramount Studios lot. She may have been a vicious killer, but she was right about one thing: Nobody's innocent.

ABOUT THE AUTHOR

A native of Toledo, Ohio, Keith Lee Johnson began writing purely by accident when a literature professor unwittingly challenged his ability to tell a credible story in class one day. He picked up a pen that very day and has been writing ever since. Upon graduating from high school in June, Keith joined the United States Air Force the following September and attained a Top Secret security clearance. He served his country in Texas, Mississippi, Nevada, California, Turkey and various other places during his four years of service. Keith has written four books and is currently working on his fifth. His next release will be *Fate's Redemption* (Summer 2005).

Sugar & Spice

BY KEITH LEE JOHNSON

AVAILABLE NOW

(ISBN 1-59309-013-7)

This fast-paced thriller twists and turns its way through the perplexing investigation of several mysterious murders that will have readers at the edge of their seats.

When a set of twins is released from prison they have one thing on their minds: to settle the score against the people who put them there in the first place. The revenge killings begin in the District of Columbia with the murder of the prison warden and his wife—both found viciously beaten and brutally dismembered—and continue on the opposite coast where a socialite is found dead in Malibu. Baffled by the gruesome murders, Detective Phoenix Perry ends her vacation early to conduct an unauthorized investigation and embarks upon a thrilling adventure to unravel the mystery and put an end to the violence.

Sugar & Spice is a gripping race to discover who is behind all of the murder, corruption and revenge, sure to keep readers guessing up to the stunning climax. From a promising new voice in fiction, this novel will keep spines tingling and pages turning.

EXCERPT FROM

Sugar & Spice

BY KEITH LEE JOHNSON

A SEQUEL TO Pretenses

CHAPTER 9

L oud music blared from the Connelly mansion, awakening the twins who had fallen asleep in the guesthouse. After a few seconds, they recognized the tune. It was Levert's "Casanova." Evidently, the party was underway. According to the digital clock resting on the fireplace mantle, it was a little after eleven. Alex picked up the high-powered binoculars and looked through the lenses toward the mansion. It looked like every light in the house was on. Alex could see Heather, Sandra, and Paula in the recreation room on the first floor.

The man that Heather had had sex with earlier was sitting in a chair, watching Paula peel off her clothing. Sandra, the natural blonde, was leaning against the eight-foot pool table watching the show. She was wearing a leopard jacket and a short black skirt that barely covered her derriere.

"You ready, Sam?" Alex asked.

"Yeah, let's go."

They grabbed their backpacks, put on a pair of surgical gloves, and walked out the door. It was dark outside, but they found their way back easily by following the paved trail past the tennis courts, past the swimming pool, and up the stairs. Suddenly the music stopped. By the time the twins finished climbing the stairs, Heather and Sandra were locked in a vise-like kiss near the pool table, ripping at each other's clothes. Paula, completely nude, was on her knees in front of the man sitting in the chair. Her head bobbed up and down rapidly like a crack whore who had been promised a vial full of the addicting drug.

The twins walked around to the front of the house. They wanted the element of surprise. When they reached the front of the mansion, they saw the red Diablo and the black Carrera GT parked in the circular driveway. Alex turned off the alarm and they entered the house undetected again. Their hearts began to pound the moment they entered the residence.

"This is going to be absolutely delicious," Alex whispered.

"I know," Sam whispered.

CHAPTER 10

Slowly, so as not to draw attention to themselves, the twins unzipped the backpacks and pulled out an Omega stun baton that was guaranteed to make even the fiercest assailant behave. The baton had one hundred fifty-thousand volts running up and down the entire unit above the handle. Any part of the baton would render an assailant unconscious. They tiptoed down the hallway past the living room, through the kitchen, and past the formal dining room.

As they approached the recreation room, they could hear the sound of raw sex emanating from the room. The sound was so distinct—so animalistic—so erotic that it aroused the twins. With their backs against the wall, they peered around the opening and saw Heather Connelly's face buried in Sandra Rhodes' blonde crotch. Sandra's black skirt was pushed up over her butt, her feet flat on the table with her legs at a forty-five-degree angle. Her surgically enlarged breasts were exposed and her leopard panties dangled on her right ankle.

The man and Paula were on the floor facing the pool in a doggy-style position. He was thrusting in what looked like an angry fury. Paula's sighs were high-pitched and rhythmic. She twisted her long neck so that she could look back at the man. Paula was a very pretty brunette with dimples and thick black arched eyebrows. Her hair was short and curled to the back.

The twins waited until Paula faced the pool again before entering the room. The couples were so absorbed in their eroticism that they had no idea the twins were there. They walked over to the bar and poured a glass of chilled chardonnay. They sat down, ate a few shrimp, some cheese and crackers, and watched the show. After a few more voyeuristic minutes, they walked over to the man and Paula.

"Having fun, kids?" Alex laughed, and lifted a champagne glass as if a toast was being offered.

The scene immediately switched from one of rampant sexual abandon to that of a deer being caught in the headlights of an oncoming car. The moaning ceased and the man pulled out of Paula. With the exception of Heather, they all scrambled to find their clothes.

"Who the hell are you?" the man asked.

"Don't worry about it," Alex told him and zapped him with the baton. Paula was about to say something and Alex zapped her also. Both of them were unconscious.

Alex walked over to the bar, picked up a towel and then walked over to Heather and threw it in her face.

"Wipe her juice off your mouth!" Alex demanded.

EXCERPT FROM

Fate's Redemption

BY KEITH LEE JOHNSON

SUMMER 2005

PROLOGUE

Westin St. Francis Hotel
San Francisco, California
The Wise Wedding Reception

The bridesmaid blasted through the reception hall doors and ran to the groom. She was so gripped by fear that her entire body shook uncontrollably and the loud music made it difficult for the groom to hear what she was saying. The groom leaned over and the woman screamed something into his ear. Then he ran out of the hall.

The groom practically knocked the doors off their hinges when he entered the nursery, where his year-old babies wailed loudly as if they knew the gravity of the situation. He saw his wife, who was bound and gagged—her eyes bulging out of her head. Her face revealed the unimaginable fear that must have filled her mind. But the wife wasn't as afraid for herself or her husband as she was for her two children, who lay in their crib, screaming for the affection they could only get from their mother.

A man was standing next to the wife with a silenced 9mm to her head. The hired nanny was lying in a pool of her own blood near the twin infants. The man had shot her in the face and chest when she tried to protect the children.

For a brief moment, the groom could hear the beating of his heart, which pounded in his chest like a jackhammer, threatening to explode. Having committed one murder, he knew the man had nothing to lose. He kept telling himself to stay calm, when everything in him wanted to wrestle the gun away from him, put it in his mouth, and fire until there were no bullets left.

The man grinned. "So glad you could make it." He had a glazed, almost vacant look in his eyes. "We've got some unfinished business—you and I."

Somehow I've got to stall him. Make him think about what he's doing. "What do you want?" the groom asked in a forced calm. He looked completely relaxed, but he was mortified. *I've gotta do something before he pulls the trigger.*

"Isn't it obvious?" The man asked with a twisted grin. "I want you to watch her die. That's what I want. As you see," he looked at the slain nanny, "I won't hesitate to kill, Doctor. I've killed eight others. I can still see their faces…" He seemed to be losing his grip on reality, but quickly gathered himself. "I'M NOT CRAZY!" The man shouted, then closed his eyes and took a deep breath, collecting himself again.

"I can't begin to tell you the rage I felt when I saw your wedding plans in The Chronicle," the man continued. "Here you two were getting married and moving on with your pathetic lives. And here I am with nothin'. No wife, no kids, no partner, nothin'. You two ruined my life. Now, do you really think I'm going to stand by and watch you two have the best of everything? I sat in there and watched you two at that altar, looking into each other eyes, saying your little vows like a '90s version of *Cinderella*. Well, you can forget about this fairy-tale ending happily ever after."

"You don't want to kill her," the groom offered calmly, trying to maintain his composure. "I'm the one you wanted to hurt that night, not her. Please, let her and the babies go, and take me."

"Do you really think I'm going to let her go so you can be Prince Valiant? DO YOU?" the man screamed. "And don't think for a moment you can get into my head and talk your way outta this. I've been planning your deaths for too long to stop now." He pulled out another 9mm and slid it across the floor. It stopped about eight inches from the groom's feet.

"Pick it up."

"Let's talk about this," the groom desperately pleaded with the man.

"That's the gun you took outta my holster that night. And this one, the one I'm holding to your pretty little wife's head, this is Sykes' gun. This way, it ends the way it was supposed to that night. Sykes would have killed you with this gun, Dr. Chaney," he told the bride. "As it stands, this same gun is going to kill you." The man looked at the groom and yelled, "PICK IT UP, WILLY!"

"You expect me to be able to pick the gun up and shoot you before you pull the trigger?"

"That's the deal, Willy. And you got ten seconds to try."

"What happened? Did your wife leave you while you were in prison?"

"Ten...Nine..."

The groom's mind raced. He was running out of time. The bride's eyes seemed to be pleading with him to go for the gun. He could hear her muffled pleas. The groom was a marksman, but with the stress of the situation he was afraid he would accidentally shoot her instead.

"What happened to you in prison?" The groom stalled. "Were you abused? Sexually assaulted?"

"Eight...Seven...Six..."

Seeing no other way out, the groom picked up the gun and squeezed the trigger...

Johnson, Keith Lee
Sugar & Spice 1-59309-013-7
Pretenses 1-59309-018-8

Johnson, Rique
Love & Justice 1-59309-002-1
Whispers From a Troubled Heart (July 2004) 1-59309-020-X
Every Woman's Man (November 2004) 1-59309-036-6
Sistergirls.com 1-59309-004-8

Lee, Darrien
All That and a Bag of Chips 0-9711953-0-7
Been There, Done That 1-59309-001-3
What Goes Around Comes Around (July 2004) 1-59309-024-2

Luckett, Jonathan
Jasminium 1-59309-007-2
How Ya Livin' 1-59309-025-0

McKinney, Tina Brooks
All That Drama (December 2004) 1-59309-033-1

Quartay, Nane
Feenin 0-9711953-7-4

Rivers, V. Anthony
Daughter by Spirit 0-9674601-4-X
Everybody Got Issues 1-59309-003-X
Sistergirls.com 1-59309-004-8

Roberts, J. Deotis
Roots of a Black Future: Family and Church 0-9674601-6-6
Christian Beliefs 0-9674601-5-8

Stephens, Sylvester
Our Time Has Come (September 2004) 1-59309-026-9

Turley II, Harold
Love's Game (November 2004) 1-59309-029-3

Valentine, Michelle
Nyagra's Falls 0-9711953-4-X

White, A.J.
Ballad of a Ghetto Poet 1-59309-009-9

White, Franklin
Money for Good 1-59309-012-9
Potentially Yours 1-59309-027-7

Zane (Editor)
Breaking the Cycle (September 2004) 1-59309-021-8